"You think I'm plain and insignificant!"

Janet protested, "You've never thought of me as a woman before! Just because I came to the rendezvous instead of my cousin, I can't be forced to take her place!"

Alex interrupted, "Presumably you have a woman's body under that unspeakable dress of yours?"

Jan's face flamed. "You're even more despicable than I thought!"

"Despicable, am I?" he snarled. "I'll teach you to call me names such as cad and pig. I intend to live up to that reputation tonight."

He seized her then, enclosing her in arms that felt like steel bands, holding her against his hard, lean body, and his mouth crushed her lips.

This must be a nightmare, Janet thought wildly.

ELIZABETH ASHTON
is also the author of these
Harlequin Romances

and this
Harlequin Presents

Many of these titles are available at your local bookseller

For a free catalogue listing all available Harlequin Romances
and Harlequin Presents, send your name and address to:

HARLEQUIN READER SERVICE
M.P.O. Box 707, Niagara Falls, NY 14302
Canadian address: Stratford, Ontario N5A 6W2

Borrowed Plumes

by

ELIZABETH ASHTON

Harlequin Books

TORONTO • LONDON • LOS ANGELES • AMSTERDAM
SYDNEY • HAMBURG • PARIS • STOCKHOLM • ATHENS • TOKYO

Original hardcover edition published in 1980
by Mills & Boon Limited

ISBN 0-373-02395-2

Harlequin edition published April 1981

CHAPTER ONE

'ALEXANDROS BEY, *hanim.*'

The little Turkish maid opened the door of the sitting room, and stood aside to permit the visitor to pass her. Though her head was bowed subserviently, as was the custom in the presence of a lordly male, her sly eyes slid sideways to watch him go by. Even humble serving girls were conscious of Alexandros Leandris' masculine magnetism.

The young woman seated in the window embrasure in front of a portable typewriter looked up but did not rise as the man paused inside the doorway, the maid having discreetly closed the door behind him. She knew it was not herself he had come to see and she resented his intrusion. She saw his glance roam round the room seeking another presence and was pleased by his disappointment. She disliked him intensely, but she had to admit that he was a striking-looking man. His bared head was covered with thick black hair that had a tendency to curl, his features were regular, and his eyes under the straight black brows were tiger's eyes, tawny and predatory, as if seeking unwary prey. His sunburned skin glowed golden brown against the white of his short-sleeved silk shirt, the muscles rippling in his smooth forearms. He was not very tall, but his lithe figure was perfectly proportioned from broad shoulders to narrow hips, and he moved with a feline grace.

But it was none of his physical attributes which were so arresting, it was his air of authority, the aura of leashed power which exuded from his whole personality from the crown of his imperious head to his well shod feet. He was an arrogant, forceful man who expected to have his own way and would be dangerous to cross, and indeed most of his associates found it expedient to give way to Alexandros Leandris, who was both wealthy and powerful.

Incongruously he was carrying a sheaf of red roses in hands which looked more fitted to handle a weapon.

'I think there must be some mistake,' he said in a deep pleasant voice in accentless English; at least it would have been pleasant if it were not so cold. 'I was told Miss Reynolds was at home.'

Equally coldly she returned, 'I am Miss Reynolds,' but there was a spark of mischief in her eyes.

'But ...' For a second his eyes rested upon her and then looked away, as if the sight of her offended him. Janet Reynolds made no effort to enhance her appearance. Since her childhood she had been overlooked in favour of her glamorous cousin so that she had come to take a perverse pleasure in emphasising her plainness. She wore no make-up, and her light brown hair was drawn back into a knot in the nape of her neck, while her cotton frock, innocent of style, clung to her boyish figure. Yet a discerning eye would have seen her possibilities. The bone structure of her face was good, a broad forehead and determined chin, a sensitive mouth, and her long narrow eyes were of an unusual shade of vivid blue. But no one ever gave her a second glance when Renata was present; her cousin's glory of red-gold hair and green eyes totally eclipsed her, and though the visitor had upon a previous occasion been introduced to her, he obviously did not remember her.

'It's Renata you've come to see, isn't it?' she said quietly. 'She happens to be my cousin.'

'Oh, yes, of course, you are staying with her here.' He turned on his charm to retrieve his blunder and his smile momentarily dispelled his habitual hauteur. 'Forgive me, Miss Reynolds, that I didn't immediately recognise you, I expected to see Renata. You act as your uncle's secretary, I believe? He must find you very helpful.'

His gaze was upon the papers spread before her and so missed her fleeting one which lit up her face with elfin charm.

'He does,' she returned gravely. 'I'm the useful member of the family, Renata is its ornament, but I'm afraid she's not at home. She has gone to Izmir for the day.'

The black brows descended in a frown. 'Again?'

Jan saw the frown with inward glee. She had overheard the row on the previous day, when Alex had called for Renata intending to go out to the ancient ruins of Ephesus where her father was working, and the girl, who took no interest in what he was doing, had wanted to be taken into Izmir, which she found more amusing than the little town of Kusadasi where they were staying. Neither had given way, and Alex had left in a huff. The roses were evidently a peace offering and he had come to be reconciled, but Renata was absent.

'Yes, again,' she confirmed. 'She finds it more lively than here,' adding with malicious satisfaction, 'Denis Wood has gone with her.'

Alex made an impatient gesture and laid the roses down on the table, muttering something uncomplimentary about the other man.

'She's very fond of him,' Jan said sweetly, adding fuel to the flame. 'It's nice to meet a countryman in this part of the world.'

Greeks are proverbially jealous, though Alex was only half Greek, his mother was English. He could more accurately be described as cosmopolitan, for there was a romantic story about a Turkish grandmother, in proof of which he had Turkish connections whose influence had helped to obtain for Mr Reynolds his present privileges. He had been partly educated in England, which accounted for his knowledge of the language, but he looked more Greek than anything else, and he had the traditional Greek love of beauty in all its forms, which had drawn him to Renata.

Renata shamelessly made use of Denis to needle him, for she was a little in awe of her impressive suitor and found the company of the British boy more relaxing. He was on holiday in Kusadasi, and was badly smitten, but since he was a very ordinary young man, Alex had not taken him seriously as a rival. This was the second time Renata had gone out with him, and at a time when she knew Alex might be calling, so she was asking for trouble.

Jan was pleased to be able to impart the information. She knew Alex was pursuing her cousin, if his lordly approach could be termed a pursuit, but she did not trust him. He had a reputation. Alexandros Leandris' name had been coupled with many beautiful women, but he had married none of them. Renata was flattered by his attentions, but Jan hoped her heart was not involved, for it was doubtful if Alex were serious. The situation was further complicated by the fact that Jeremy Reynolds was under an obligation to the Greek. He had obtained for him in spite of opposition from the Turks a commission to construct a model of ancient Ephesus as it had appeared in its heyday for the museum at Istanbul. This entailed lengthy visits to the site, measuring and drawing sketches of the existing ruins to be reconstructed. The girls had accompanied him for a holiday, staying in a villa in nearby Kusadasi, whence he returned every night. His wife disliked foreign places and had stayed at home.

Janet had been orphaned when very young, and her aunt and uncle had brought her up with their own child who was the same age. She had taken a secretarial course so that she could help her uncle with his books and pamphlets; he was an authority on classical architecture. But Renata, who expected to marry young, was untrained for anything at all. Alex had met her at a party in London, and this commission offered to her father had been the outcome.

Jeremy Reynolds, being innocent and trusting, suspected no ulterior motive, but he was not so unworldly that it had not occurred to him that Alex would be a wonderful match for his daughter. He was proud of her beauty and had always spoiled her; he considered she was fit to mate with a prince, which in a sense Alex was, having succeeded to a vast shipping empire at a comparatively early age.

Jan instinctively mistrusted him, but her hints fell upon deaf ears; both father and daughter were convinced he meant marriage. Although she had been brought up in its shadows, Jan did not resent Renata's beauty, she loved and admired her cousin and expected to take a back seat when she was around. Renata was a gorgeous butterfly destined for a brilliant marriage, while Jan was an inferior creature plodding in her wake who probably would never marry at all. But she was determined that when this holiday in Kusadasi was over she would launch out on her own and support herself by her own earnings.

Alex had appeared in Kusadasi almost as soon as they had arrived in his yacht on the pretext of seeing how Jeremy was progressing. The boat was anchored below their windows and a perpetual reminder of his presence.

It soon became obvious that the real object of his visit was Renata, and Jan viewed his coming with apprehension. Even if his intentions were honest, she thought he was too proud and overbearing to make her cousin happy, and though Renata was dazzled by him, she was not in love with him, or so it appeared to Jan, who admitted she was not exactly an authority on the subject, but all her instincts were suspicious of the man.

She was glad that this morning Renata was out with another man, though she feared it was only a temporary respite, but it was just possible the proud Greek might take umbrage at her cousin's seeming preference for the Englishman. She said innocently:

'Denis is so devoted to her.'

'More fool he,' Alex growled. 'She's only making use of him.'

He was examining the contents of the room, which was adequately but not luxuriously furnished. As it was on a rise its wide window presented a good view of the sea and the low hills to the right of it. A long esplanade bordered the water to which cruise ships were moored or sent their tenders to land their passengers. Since it was a favourite port of call there was nearly always one and sometimes two of these floating hotels off the coast.

'Oh, I don't know.' Jan was deliberately trying to provoke him. 'He's a nice boy and very obliging. Rena appreciates that.'

'Meaning he does what she wants and I don't?'

'Beauty is privileged,' Jan told him softly.

Alex moved impatiently towards the window.

'Rubbish! I refuse to be any woman's footstool. Your cousin is a capricious spitfire who needs taming.'

He must be needled to be so ungallant, Jan reflected. She murmured:

'Not surprising she prefers Denis.'

He swung round and glared at her.

'Did you say *preferred*?'

'I did.'

He laughed scornfully and returned his gaze to the scene outside.

'My good girl, you're being naïve. Women have only contempt for the men they can twist round their fingers. They need to be dominated, that is the male's prerogative.'

Jan felt a cold trickle run down her spine. This arrogant man was ruthless, he would take what he wanted regardless of the feelings of others. She was feminine enough herself to sense his powerful sexual magnetism, and she trembled for Renata who might become his victim. She wondered if her uncle was aware of his dangerous potential. Jeremy was a very easy-going man, absorbed in his work and reluctant to believe ill of others. Besides, Alex might be serious, Renata was very lovely and presumably he would need a wife some time to produce an heir to his kingdom as he was past his first youth, but would he be kind to her?

As he continued to stare out of the window, she had ample opportunity to study his classic profile. It was undoubtedly handsome, but so hard. Was he capable of loving a woman? Did he have any affection for Renata beyond a desire to possess her beauty? Those close shut lips with their satirical curve did not look as if they could ever express tenderness. Could marriage with him be anything more than bondage? She said coolly:

'Your views are old-fashioned, Mr Leandris. Women are recognised nowadays to have equal rights with men. Your talk of domination is distasteful, in fact you seem to be qualifying for the Women's Lib definition of chauvinist pig.'

She did not care if she was being rude, his whole bearing antagonised her.

He turned his head and surveyed her out of cruel cat's eyes with a gleam in their amber depths.

'The plain woman's consolation,' he jeered. 'They abuse what they cannot hope to experience. I have never found a woman I desired resentful of my dominance.'

Jan winced inwardly. She had asked for it, but his words hurt. No woman likes to be told she is undesirable, though she knew she had never aroused such feelings in a male breast, nor was she ever likely to do so with Renata around, but she was resigned to that, and the last thing she would want to happen was to awake amatory interest in her companion; the mere suggestion was unnerving ... and ludicrous.

'Perhaps you're attracted to doormats,' she said pertly.

'Far from it, I like a woman to have spirit——' The tawny eyes glinted. 'A challenge to subdue. You couldn't call Renata a doormat.'

Emboldened by her anxiety for her cousin, Jan burst out impulsively:

'Oh, please, Mr Leandris, do leave her alone!'

He smiled derisively. 'Jealous?'

'Good lord, no, but I love Rena, I want her to be happy.'

'You think I will make her unhappy?'

Jan clasped her hands appealingly. 'I'm afraid you might.'

'Suppose you mind your own business?' he returned coldly.

'But Rena is my business,' she protested. 'She's young ... and reckless. With her father away so much I feel ...'

'If he's appointed you her guardian,' he cut in, 'you're a very ineffective one. Why are you here and not chaperoning her in Izmir?'

'Because ... because ...' Jan turned her head away. Impossible to tell him she felt no qualms about Denis, whereas she considered Alex was a menace. Unfortunately she had very little influence over Renata.

He eyed her indifferently, then said carelessly:

'You take your duties too seriously. Though in Greece young girls are still protected, the modern freedom you've been advocating has dispensed with such supervision in your country. Renata is very decorative,

I enjoy taking her out, but you being an unsophisticated virgin imagine seduction in every male approach. I advise you to find a man of your own ... if you can ... to teach you about men and life.'

Jan clenched her hands in her lap to restrain an angry outburst. There was enough truth in what he said to hurt. She had been a fool to plead with him for Renata, she had only exposed herself to mockery. She was not responsible for Renata, but being Greek he would expect a young girl to have some sort of duenna, and he probably thought she was a great deal older than her years.

'Your Renata is well able to look after herself,' he went on, 'and if she appreciates the company of a pig ... I think that was your name for me ... why should you feel called upon to interfere?'

Jan flushed. 'I'm sorry, I didn't mean to be rude ...'

'I'm perfectly aware of what you meant, Miss Reynolds. I apologise for interrupting your work.' He glanced at the papers strewn before her and moved towards the door. 'I'm sure it is more suited to your talents than trying to interpret male motives, a subject about which you're profoundly ignorant. *Adio.*'

He was gone, moving with lithe pantherish strides, leaving the roses on the table. Janet's heart swelled with loathing, she would like to have hurled them after him. But roses are living things and they did not deserve such treatment. She stood up, intending to put them in water; no reason why they should wither because their donor was a chauvinist pig.

Renata came back from her expedition with her arms full of parcels. She had been shopping, she said. Renata always seemed to shop when she went anywhere and much of what she bought was worthless. It seemed to be a compulsion with her and she could not afford the more expensive articles. She came in like a sunburst, her vivid hair gleaming, her eyes alight with the joy of living. Her green sun dress revealed plenty of matt white skin upon which the sun had little effect. Her small feet were encased in white sandals at the end of a very beautiful pair of legs. She was, as Alex had said, decorative. She had not asked Denis to come in, she announced, because ... her eyes fell on the roses.

'Did he bring those?'

'If you mean Mr Leandris, he did,' Jan told her.

'So he's been here. I thought he might have waited.' Which was why Denis had been dismissed. A strange expression came into the green eyes, triumph mingled with ... was it fear? 'But why so formal, darling? We all call him Alex.'

'I'm only on formal terms with him,' Jan said stiffly.

Renata shrugged her shoulders. 'That's your trouble, you try to keep everyone at arm's length. I hope he came to apologise.'

'He didn't seem at all apologetic.'

'No, I suppose that was too much to expect. He told me once he never explained nor apologised. You told him I was out with Denis?'

'I did.'

Renata looked eager. 'How did he take it?'

'I don't think he was pleased.'

'Did he threaten to stick knives into him or anything exciting?'

'No. He has only contempt for poor Denis.'

Renata looked disappointed. 'I hoped he'd be wild with jealousy.'

'I can't imagine Mr Leandris being wild about anything,' Jan observed drily. 'He's far too superior to be swayed by ordinary emotions, but is it fair to try to play them off against each other? I fancy if Mr Leandris were really provoked he might be a very unpleasant person to deal with.'

Again a flicker of fear in Renata's eyes. 'He's altogether too sure of himself ... and me,' she complained.

Jan sighed. 'You're playing with fire.'

'That's what's so thrilling.' Renata's green eyes sparkled. 'But don't you think Alex is wonderful?'

'I think he's hateful!'

Renata laughed merrily. 'I suppose he didn't waste any of his charm upon you, he'd have found you a poor substitute for me. Oh, I didn't mean to be unkind, but look at you, you won't even try to make the most of yourself.'

'No one ever looks at me when you're around, so why bother?' Jan spoke without rancour, it was a fact of life she had become accustomed to. Renata was eyeing the roses reflectively.

'I expect they're his way of making amends, and I'll have to thank him for them. Did he say he'd call again?'

'No.'

'Darling, you seem hipped,' commented Renata. 'Was he nasty to you?'

'I was to him. I called him a chauvinist pig.'

'Oh!' Renata clapped her hands to her mouth and stared at her cousin. 'Did you really? But what on earth did he say to cause you to say that?'

'Oh, he discoursed about male dominance in a lordly way that needled me. Rena, that man regards women as inferior beings, he has a harem mentality. If you married him ...'

'Ssh! Renata flushed and glanced around her uneasily. 'He hasn't mentioned marriage ... yet.'

'So I gathered.'

'You seem to have had quite a heart-to-heart.' Renata looked at her cousin suspiciously. 'You understand it's early days yet. I hope you didn't put your foot in it.'

Jan smiled wryly. Renata would be furious if she knew that she had dared to beg Alex to leave her alone. She looked searchingly into the beautiful, glowing face.

'Are you in love with him?' she asked bluntly.

Renata hesitated. 'I ... I'm not sure. He fascinates me, and I'm proud to have attracted him, you know how women run after him, but I'm a little scared of him. It would be marvellous to be married to him.' She turned over her purchases. 'Then I could buy all the lovely expensive things I want instead of this trash, and I should be envied for having such a handsome husband.'

'Not very good reasons for marrying,' Jan observed drily.

'I suppose you believe in undying love and all that sentimental nonsense,' Renata said contemptuously. 'That only exists between the pages of a novel, I'm down to earth, and out to make a good bargain. Of course he'll adore me, but that's different.' She smiled complacently.

Jan began to put her papers together.

'Have you thought that his intentions may not be

honourable?' she asked diffidently.

'They probably aren't,' Renata returned coolly. 'Oh, I know what's said about him, but I'm sure I can bring him up to scratch. But even if I can't ...' Her voice trailed away as she unwrapped one of her parcels which contained a gaudy necklace, a gilt ball studded with imitation turquoises. She held it up to the light wrinkling her straight little nose disdainfully. 'Cheap muck!'

Jan looked at her lovely, petulant face, her slim but rounded figure. She looked seductive enough to achieve her aim, but recalling Alex's dark arrogance, his scornful words, she felt chilled, for she doubted her cousin was capable of handling him. Wasn't it more probable he would bend her to his will? Renata was not nearly as strong-minded as she sounded, and Alex had much to offer her apart from his hand in marriage.

'Of course Denis is the nicer character,' Renata went on musingly, 'but he hasn't a bean, or only very few. Daddy hopes I'll marry Alex because then he may give him some more commissions.'

Jan was shocked. 'But he wouldn't put that before your happiness!' she gasped.

'Why shouldn't I be happy with Alex?' Renata countered.

'Because he'll bully you,' Jan told her shortly. 'You wouldn't be able to call your soul your own, and he'd probably be unfaithful.'

Renata's beautiful eyes widened fearfully.

'Nonsense,' she said quickly. 'You've taken against him because his ideas are a bit old-fashioned. He's not a Turk, though I believe he did have a Turkish grandmother, and he was educated at an English school, so he *seems* English to me.'

'Officially he's Greek, and Greeks still expect to govern their wives,' Jan pointed out.

'So what? A clever woman can get round any man if she's subtle enough,' Renata said loftily. 'You don't understand how to manage men, Jan, you're too out-spoken.'

'At least I'm honest, and I'm not mercenary,' Janet declared, piqued by this criticism.

'And you think I am——' Renata asked. She moved to the window seat and gazed out pensively at the view. Keeping her head averted, she burst out:

'Jan, I don't intend to be poor all my life. Oh, I know Daddy's got quite an adequate income, but I want to be rich. I want to have Jaguars, mink coats and diamonds. Alex has already given me this.'

She pulled on the chain she wore around her neck and drew up from between her breasts a pendant she had thus concealed. She raised the gold chain over her head and held it out to Jan. The precious stones sparkled in the sunlight, an emerald set among dia-monds.

Jan recoiled from it as if it had been a snake.

'Rena, you mustn't accept gifts like that! It must be very valuable.'

'Don't be stuffy.' Renata put on the chain again and pushed the jewels into her bodice. 'Since I've been blessed with good looks you can't blame me for cashing in on them.'

'But Rena, to accept jewels, you know what it means?'

'Pooh, that pendant is no more to Alex than an ornament from Woolworths. It was a memento of a pleasant evening out, he said. That's all.'

She stood up, walked across to the jar of roses and sniffed at the velvet petals.

'Mmm, delicious. I believe Alex is very generous to his mistresses.'

'Rena!' Jan sprang to her feet. 'You wouldn't ...?'

'Wouldn't I?' The green eyes gleamed like the emerald in the pendant. 'Darling, don't be so terribly moral, it's so dated. Of course I'd rather be Mrs Leandris, but I'm not going to lose Alex for want of a certificate. He's generous, he's willing to pay for what he wants, and I'm worth a high price.'

'You're joking, of course,' Jan said quietly. She could excuse a girl giving herself for love, but still clung to her old-fashioned belief that love should wait for the church's blessing, to make it into a sacrament. But for Renata to barter her virginity for jewels was unthinkable. Her cousin often talked in this vein without meaning a word of it, partly Jan was aware in the hope of shocking her; she assured herself she was doing so now.

Renata gave her a very naughty look, then she laughed.

'Of course I was. You're so prim and proper, Jan, I can't resist teasing you. I can't return the pendant, Alex would be furious.' Again she looked scared. 'But I'm sure he didn't mean anything wrong.'

'Then why don't you wear it openly?'

'Because Daddy would jump to conclusions, and we aren't engaged ... yet. If Alex lets me down I can always fall back on Denis.'

Jan had noticed her scared look. 'You might be happier with him. He's a nice boy.'

'He hasn't the guts to be anything else,' Renata said scornfully. 'He treats me like a kind of goddess. Isn't that sweet?'

'It's as it should be,' Jan told her severely.

'But so dull. Since he can't afford to marry, and he says he loves me, you'd think he would at least make improper advances.'

'I'd think no such thing. Like me, he perhaps still has ideals.'

Renata put her head upon one side considering her cousin through narrowed lids.

'Jan dear, you're way out of touch with modern trends,' she said sweetly. 'It's easy to preach virtue when you've never been tempted. I don't suppose you ever will be, I can't imagine you falling in love, or anyone being crazy about you. Never mind,' as Jan looked a little hurt. 'We can't all be glamorous and people like you are so necessary to keep the wheels turning. When I've gone, for of course I'll marry somebody, you can look after Daddy.'

'I'll be very glad to do that.' Jan was grateful to her uncle for giving her a home, but such a future was not very exciting. It was true she had never been in love and could not conceive of herself being swayed by strong passion so that she forgot her principles, but she was only twenty-one, far too young to accept spinsterhood as inevitable. Renata had often declared that she was a born old maid when her fastidiousness irritated her, but Jan had had her girlish dreams of a possible lover. If and when he appeared she was quite sure he would be the antithesis of Alexandros Leandris.

CHAPTER TWO

ALEX came again on the following morning and Renata greeted him with profuse thanks for his lovely flowers and regrets for having missed him on the previous day. She chose to ignore their tiff, evidently considering a reconciliation was due. If she had expected reproaches for her desertion, which was meant to mark his displeasure, she was disappointed, for he never mentioned it, nor did he make any reference to Denis. Watching them from the balcony outside the sitting room window, whence she had retreated, Jan saw his mouth curl sardonically at Renata's placatory efforts and the predatory gleam in his eyes. He knew his prey was hooked, and he could brush aside her puny efforts to assert herself.

He had given Jan a brief nod and a curt 'Good morning,' when he came into the room, his glance going immediately to Renata, and she had promptly withdrawn. He told Renata he proposed driving out to Ephesus to see how her father was progressing, and though she grimaced, Renata made no protest, fearing she had gone too far with her Izmir expedition. There was something very uncompromising about Alex's attitude that morning, which warned her to be acquiescent. To the surprise of both girls, he demanded that Jan should accompany them.

'You should have a female companion,' he told Renata. 'There are men on the site well known to me, and as your father's daughter you must be circumspect.'

'Oh, stuff!' Renata said rudely. 'I've been out alone with you before.'

'Without witnesses,' he observed. 'The men working there are mostly Turkish, and we must preserve appearances in front of them.'

'But I'm British,' Renata pointed out with a spurt of defiance. 'Why must I fall in with stupid foreign conventions?'

Alex said nothing, he merely looked at her, and her opposition melted.

'Oh, very well,' she agreed. 'Jan will enjoy it, she likes ruins.'

For the expedition Renata changed into a flimsy dress of patterned blue nylon over a silk slip. Jan remained as she was, clad in brown trousers and a cream knitted top. It suited her much better than her usual limp cotton dresses, she looked slim and boyish and the white linen hat she wore—such headgear was sold everywhere for tourists who had underestimated the heat of the sun—concealed her severe hair style and gave her a puckish air. Renata eyed her a little wistfully.

'I'd love to wear pants, they're much more suitable for this sort of expedition, but Alex hates them on a woman. He wants me to look feminine, as he puts it.'

'Well, thank goodness I don't have to dress to please him,' Jan remarked. 'But you should be more independent, Rena, you're not engaged to him yet.'

'But I want him to admire me,' Renata retorted, 'not look at me with repugnance.'

Jan assured herself not very successfully that she

did not care how repugnant she appeared to Alex, and in any case he never seemed to notice her to approve or disapprove, so it really did not matter what she wore. But upon this occasion he did, for when he came to collect them and the maid showed him in, he kissed Renata's fingertips with one of his flowery compliments which always sounded to Jan to be so insincere, then turned to her cousin. The strange cat's eyes surveyed her from top to toe with a curious intentness. Jan might be too slim, but she was graceful, and her long legs were flattered by her outfit, although she was lacking in curves.

'I must apologise, Miss Reynolds,' he said with a slight drawl. 'I see I was mistaken about you, you are very much younger than I took you for. You're not much more than a child.'

Jan flushed angrily. First he considered her to be a desiccated spinster, now he thought she was an adolescent!

'I'm the same age as Rena,' she said shortly.

'Really?' He glanced admiringly at Renata's rounded limbs. Later she might need to watch her weight, but at that time she was just right. 'A case of arrested development,' he murmured.

Apparently an aside, Jan knew he had meant her to hear. He was retaliating for her chauvinist pig. She flushed angrily.

'Do you have to be insulting?' she flashed, her eyes intensely blue. 'Hitherto you've hardly been able to bring yourself to look at me, now do you have to be rude?'

'Oh, I don't think he meant to be,' Renata intervened hastily. 'But you do look more like a boy than a girl in that get-up, and very young.' She looked archly at Alex. 'It's fashionable to be flat as a board, but I know you prefer curves.'

'I certainly like a woman to look like a woman,' he agreed. 'I didn't mean to insult you, Miss Reynolds. I was taken aback to see that Renata's chaperone looks more in need of a guardian herself.'

'Oh, come off it, Alex,' Renata cried irritably. 'Guardians and chaperones are dead as the dodo. We aren't like your Greek women who expect to be provided for and cherished, we're independent modern girls—and for heaven's sake call her Jan!'

Alex smiled, the attractive smile that so altered his face.

'With your permission, Jan, I'll be charmed to do so,' he said gallantly.

Her name on his lips gave Jan a quite unexpected pleasure, and she had to admit that his smile was devastating when she was the recipient of it. Mollified, she told him:

'Please do, and I apologise for my prickles. You and I seem to rub each other up the wrong way.'

'Chauvinist pig,' he murmured, and there was a glint of humour in his eyes.

'That was most uncalled for,' Renata cried wrathfully.

Alex shrugged his shoulders. 'She was not flattering, but after a surfeit of sugar, vinegar can be stimulating. Shall we go?'

His remark pleased neither girl. Renata feared he might be finding her cloying, and Jan would rather have his indifference than his interest.

The ruins of Ephesus lie along a valley between two

hills, Mount Pion and Mount Koressos. The famous temple that was once one of the seven wonders of the ancient world was situated outside its walls in the village of Selcuk. In those days the sea washed its steps and reflected its honey-coloured pillars, and also filled the city harbour, for Ephesus was a thriving seaport. Now the sea has retreated four miles away and all that is left of the magnificent temple is a solitary pillar (reconstructed) and a few stones lying in a marshy pool; a number of the others were shipped to Istanbul to adorn the interior of St Sophia.

Ephesus had been pagan, Christian and Islamic. Above the site of the pagan temple is the basilica of St John, and St John's tomb—there is quite a lot of that still standing—and further up the hill, enclosed by Byzantine walls, a mosque. The excursion coaches stop at the massive stone gate leading into the ruins, and when due respect has been paid to the Saint, they continue to where the old city begins, drop their passengers, and meet them again at its further end. It is quite a long walk, for Ephesus was a big city, down through the piles of ruined masonry, some of which like the portico of the Temple of Trajan and the Library have been reconstructed. Downhill past the Upper Agora, the visitor walks, along the street of the Curetes, where on the left five-storied terraced houses once stood, now exposed to their cellars, along the marble street, and it is marble, to the huge amphitheatre, past baths and brothels, and finally turning at a right angle, along Harbour Street flanked by the broken pillars of the Lower Agora, the market place, which leads to the flat plain that was once part of the sparkling Aegean Sea. It is a ghost city, originally

Greek, but Rome and Byzantium have left their mark, but the statues and valuables that once adorned it have been taken to the museums of Izmir and Istanbul to preserve them.

A road leads off Harbour Street to a parking place, and it was at that point that Alex left his car on that lovely morning. Renata immediately flew to the souvenir shops, of which there were many clustering round the entrance to the town. Alex and Jan followed her more leisurely and Alex stopped to make a purchase at a stall. It was a miniature replica of the goddess whose statue had once adorned the vanished temple, several copies of which had been excavated. He presented it to Renata with a flourish.

'Diana of the Ephesians, madame.'

Renata stared with distaste at the quaint figurine with its breastplate of what looked like a mass of oval eggs.

'But I thought she was classical, the moon goddess, a graceful figure with a crescent in her hair.'

'So the Greeks pictured her, but Ephesus had a polyglot population. Their Artemis became confused with a fertility goddess, the original Earth Mother of the earlier cults. She was more fundamental than moon nymphs. After all, that is what most men marry for—progeny.'

He was warning Renata what would be expected of her if he married her, but from her expression it was not her idea at all. There was a teasing light in the golden eyes, but she did not see it. She was staring in disgust at the effigy. Jan momentarily envisioned tall golden-skinned sons with dark wavy hair. Surely that would be an achievement of which any woman would be proud? But Renata was not a maternal type. She made as if to throw the figure away, then, catching Alex's sardonic eye, dropped it into her handbag.

'We'd better find Daddy,' she said coldly. 'That's what we've come for, isn't it?'

Alex enquired of a guide at the gate, who waved vaguely towards the hillside above the city.

'He's up by the old walls,' Alex told them. 'As I can't bring my car in here, you'll have to walk, I'm afraid.'

Jan was agreeable, though Renata pouted. She set off gaily along the broad road, leaving the other two to follow. The sky above them was a clear blue, the surrounding hills were gently rounded shapes of green and brown where sheep grazed. It was a pastoral peaceful scene where the streams of tourists were dwarfed by its spaciousness and the vastness of the ruined town. Up the broad steps into Marble Street, turning right past the Library of Celsus, the most ambitious piece of reconstruction so far, and uphill, where the ruined houses leaned on the slopes of Mount Koressos. Here where the partially restored Temple of Hadrian lifted a magnificent arch into the blue sky, Renata came to a halt.

'How much farther do you expect me to go?' she demanded, for her high-heeled sandals were quite unequal to the terrain. 'My feet are killing me!'

Alex silently pointed upwards where above a flight of steps, to the side of the temple, was a view of the hillside and a stretch of the Byzantine wall that had once enclosed the city. Leaning against it, binoculars in hand, was a white-clad figure crowned by a panama hat—Jeremy Reynolds.

'I'm not going up there,' Renata said firmly. She sat

down on a marble block, spreading her skirts around her. 'Perhaps he'll come down if you shout.'

'I'll fetch him.' Jan shot away like an arrow up the steps and threading her way between blocks of stone and pillars, out on to the hillside. It was very steep and rough going, but she had the sure-footed agility of a goat. Suddenly she became aware that Alex was beside her. She stopped, troubled by his presence; he was a disruptive element in a place which always stimulated her imagination, and she wanted to be alone with her fancies. From the hilltop she could reconstruct the once prosperous city in her mind's eye and dream herself back into the past, as she had hoped to do, once she had delivered her message to her uncle.

'I wonder you dare leave Rena,' she told him.

They both looked down at the seated figure. A party of young Americans was straggling past her, the masculine half of it finding her more interesting than the ruins. Even from a distance her complacent attitude was discernible; she was enjoying their admiring glances. Alex's expression was indifferent.

'She won't run away, and a man likes his property to be appreciated.'

Jan threw him a questioning glance. 'So you consider she's your property? Are you engaged?'

'We're not, but she's mine for the asking.'

'Then you ought to be,' Jan said severely. 'You've no right to play fast and loose with her affections, Mr Leandris ...'

He held up his hand to check her.

'Spare me your recriminations, miss. We had words upon this subject before and it bores me. You're not your cousin's keeper, and it's her father's place to ask me my intentions, not yours.'

He was quite insufferable, Jan decided. Only her acute anxiety on Renata's behalf had prompted her words, words which would have been better unspoken. Her uncle would never question Alex's motives. He had convinced himself they were all they should be, and he had not seen the diamond pendant.

With her cheeks burning from his rebuff, Jan sped away from him up the hillside, but Alex soon overtook her and with ease.

'No reason to give yourself a coronary because you don't like home truths,' he said derisively. 'That won't do anyone any good.'

She came to a halt, noting with annoyance that while her exertions had left her breathless, Alex showed no sign of strain. He must be in excellent physical condition, she admitted grudgingly. Indulgence had not impaired it—but was he self-indulgent? She was judging by his fine yacht and big car; he might work very hard to earn them for all she knew, though he seemed to have had plenty of leisure since they had come to Kusadasi.

'You're wondering how a man in my position manages to keep fit,' he stated. 'I'm an abstemious eater and I take a lot of exercise.'

She was disconcerted that he seemed able to guess her thoughts, and she said coldly:

'I'm not really very interested in your way of life, Mr Leandris.'

'Then you ought to be, as I'm a prospective suitor for Renata's hand, but you'll never get a husband if you don't control that tongue of yours.'

'Nor am I particularly interested in getting a husband,' she retorted, 'but do you mean you *are* serious about Renata?'

'Definitely so, but there are other relationships between men and women besides matrimony.'

Jan turned away and began to plod steadily upward. His last sentence was ominous, and she knew she could not influence her cousin. Renata would go her wilful way regardless of consequences, and even her father couldn't control her. Was it any use trying to warn him?

'And don't you go telling tales to Daddy,' Alex told her, catching her thought with an almost uncanny rapport. Rapport with this forbidding stranger? Absurd idea. 'He won't be sympathetic.'

'No, you've taken care of that,' she said bitterly, and stumbled over a stone. He caught her arm to steady her, and a quiver ran through her at the contact of his lean brown fingers with her bare arm. It was not distaste, but an electric tingling of her nerves. Damn the man!—she could feel his magnetic attraction much as she disliked and distrusted him.

'Thank you,' she muttered, and rubbed her arm where he had held it.

He said: 'You have a soft skin, smooth as satin.'

That was so unexpected that she gaped at him.

'Did you expect it to be prickly?'

'Outside as well as in?' His smile was devastating, lighting up the hard planes of his face, and displaying even white teeth. 'You're not a hedgehog.'

'I'm afraid I am a bit thorny at times,' she admitted. 'But Rena's a sore subject.'

'Then suppose you leave it alone.'

She sighed. 'I haven't much option, but oh, I wish we'd never met you.'

'Another prick?' He grinned. 'But if you hadn't, you wouldn't have come to Kusadasi. Aren't you enjoying your visit?'

It was on the tip of her tongue to retort, 'Very much, if it weren't for you,' but she bit the words back; he was impervious to her rudeness, and she had done Renata no good. Again he guessed her thought.

'I'm afraid I'm the serpent in your Eden,' he observed.

'Since you say so, you are, but it's not me you're tempting.'

He gave her a sly look.

'It might come to that. You're quite fetching in your boy's clothes.'

Incorrigible flirt, she thought, he had to try to charm even her unprepossessing self when no other woman was present. She said coolly:

'I'm impervious to flattery, Mr Leandris, and you know you consider I'm a dowd, if not next door to a freak.'

'You're mistaken, and no woman is indifferent to compliments, unless you're quite exceptional.'

'Oh, I am,' she declared. 'Didn't you know, I'm unique!'

Which piece of bravado brought them up to Jeremy, who was fiddling with his camera and his field glasses. He was a spare man, of medium height, with hair and small beard of a ginger hue. His eyes were green like his daughter's.

'Wonderful birds' eye view of the place from up here,' he said to Alex as if his appearance was expected.

'Has it ever struck you, my boy, how pervasive the female element is in Ephesus? First it was famous for its worship of Diana, the goddess's temple was the focal centre of the district, then St John was reputed to have brought the Virgin Mary here. That is her supposed house over there ...' He swung his glasses to focus it. 'Nice little church they've built, and a fine statue. The natives, I fancy, identified her with Artemis.'

'Don't we all worship lovely womanhood?' Alex asked solemnly, but with a mischievous glint in his eyes.

Jeremy looked at him suspiciously.

'I don't believe you worship anything,' he said bluntly, 'and your lady friends adore *you*.' He suddenly noticed Jan. 'What are you doing here? Where's Rena?'

'She stayed down below, she couldn't face the climb,' Alex explained, 'but this niece of yours skipped up like a chamois.'

'Jan was always a bit of a tomboy,' Jeremy remarked absently. 'Now about this model, it's to be of the original Greek city, of course ...'

As the two men became engrossed in talk, Jan wandered away over the short turf. She felt disturbed. Not only had Alex been able to read her thoughts, but she was dismayed by the effect his touch had upon her senses. Dimly she glimpsed forces within herself the existence of which she had not suspected. Modern literature is full of descriptions of passionate urges and the responses they elicit in the opposite sex, but she had had no personal experience of such emotions, she had not even suffered from schoolgirl crushes. As a teenager she had been shy and awkward with boys,

while grown men filled her with awe. Her uncle was
the only male she had ever known intimately, and she
was all the more vulnerable because her sexual feelings had been repressed. That Alexandros Leandris of
all people should be the agent to stir her sleeping
womanhood was sheer disaster. She disliked the man
intensely, believing him to be arrogant and overbearing, though his position offered some excuse. A man
could not rule a vast mercantile empire without becoming despotic, and she could not deny that he had physical charm. She had an uneasy suspicion that if he ever
turned it on in her direction, she might succumb to it.
She had no wish to join the ranks of his adorers to
which her uncle had jeeringly referred. But she was
quite safe; Renata was Alex's objective, and he had
only talked to her today because she happened to be
beside him. Unconsciously she sighed.

Unwillingly her eyes kept turning towards the bulky
remnant of the old Byzantine wall that had once encircled the city beside which the two men were talking
earnestly. Her gaze lingered on Alex's lithe figure. No
man had any right to be so good-looking, she decided;
it was not fair to his female acquaintances. He wore
neither hat or sunglasses, the strong sunlight did not
seem to affect him. His short-sleeved casual shirt
showed the strong column of his throat, his brown neck,
and his sunburned arms. His hands were thrust into his
trouser pockets as he idly kicked at a stone while he
conversed. Even standing at a distance, she caught his
aura of leashed power. Occasionally he glanced towards her, but she did not think he really saw her.

With another sigh she turned to look for Renata,
who was visible in miniature down below. One of the

bolder of the tourist youths had engaged her in conversation and she was laughing and talking animatedly. Jan glanced fearfully at Alex. Had he seen? Apparently not, for he appeared to be quite unconcerned. But that might be a mask for his real feelings. She decided she had better go down and break up the party before he vented his displeasure upon her cousin. He had not approved of the Izmir expedition with Denis Wood. She scrambled down the steep hillside and as she came nearer she recognized the youth as Denis. Had he come by chance or had Renata found a means to let him know where they were going before they set out? She was foolish to incense Alex further by encouraging him, but perhaps she did care for him after all, and he would persuade her to throw off the dark spell the man by the Byzantine wall had woven about her. That would be a wonderful solution of her cousin's future, Jan thought as a block of buildings obscured her view of the couple, but when she had negotiated her way back on to the road, Denis had gone and Renata was demurely sitting alone.

'What an age you've been,' she complained as Jan came up to her. 'I'm bored to death!'

'But you had company,' Jan pointed out.

'So you saw?' Renata giggled. 'You can't blame me if Alex goes off and leaves me alone. So lucky Denis was passing.' She looked sharply at her cousin. 'You seemed to be having quite a flirt with Alex of your own up there.'

'Oh, don't be ridiculous,' Jan said crossly, hoping she had not blushed. Her arm still tingled where Alex had grasped it. 'As if he'd look at me!'

'He was looking at you, though it may have been

with revulsion,' Renata drawled, 'and he seemed in no hurry to shake you off. Don't trespass, darling, he's my property.'

'He considers you're his.'

Renata smiled complacently. 'So he told you that, and my warning was unnecessary.' She stretched her shapely legs. 'This stone is hard. I fancy it won't be long before Alex publicises his claim.'

'That'll be a relief,' said Jan, although she felt misgivings. But once Renata and Alex were officially engaged there would be no danger of the alternative, and their marriage might turn out all right. Her flighty cousin needed to be controlled and might not resent being dominated if she had plenty of money to spend. Jan believed that a happy marriage depended upon partnership, a sharing of each other's lives, and she could not see Renata sharing interests with Alex, but she probably would not want to do so. She was sure that the Greek held women in contempt though he was dependent upon them for his pleasure. Perhaps that was why; they were too eager to oblige him and accept what he offered. Renata's motives, she feared, were more mercenary than loving too, but Alex seemed generous enough. Not an ideal union, but perhaps it would work. She gave a long sigh as she flopped down on the block of stone beside her cousin.

'You've tired yourself scrambling up that hill,' Renata said more kindly. 'You should have stayed with me. That's what Alex expected you to do.'

'I didn't anticipate he'd come after me. I was going to tell your father to come down here to you.'

If she had stayed put she would not have had that moment of revelation. Absently she stroked her arm.

'People never do what you expect them to, do they, Jan?' Renata remarked with a hint of malice. 'They fall short of your ideals and so you're always being let down. Thank goodness I haven't got any. Ah, here's Alex.' She stood up shaking out her skirts. 'I thought you'd deserted me.'

'That is impossible,' he said gallantly, but strangely his eyes were upon Jan. 'Your young cousin seemed determined to break her neck by her precipitous descent.'

Knowing that she had hurried to warn Denis off, Jan looked uncomfortable.

'Oh, Jan's always so impetuous,' Renata said carelessly.

'Now you do surprise me, I believed Jan's actions were always premeditated. Even her haste just now had a reason.'

So he had seen and recognised Denis. Jan glanced at him nervously, expecting an explosion, but he remained calm and suave. Possibly he considered a young man who fled at his approach was a poor creature and need not be feared as a rival. The significance of his last remark had not penetrated Renata's intelligence, for she said brightly:

'If you've finished with Dad, let's go somewhere more amusing. I'm sick of staring at those stones.'

'You're hard to please, madame,' Alex observed drily. 'People come half way across the globe to stare at the stones of Ephesus.'

'Probably they weren't brought up on ruins like we were,' Renata retorted. 'Pompeii, Crete—Dad's crazy about the lot, but Jan and I prefer something modern.'

Alex turned quizzical eyes in Jan's direction.

'Do you share your cousin's views, chamois?'

Jan hesitated. She didn't, but she did not want to support Alex. Renata caught at the name he had called her and saved her the necessity of a reply.

'Chamois?'

'She's as surefooted as a goat, but chamois sounds prettier.'

'If we're going to have a menagerie—pigs and goats, what do I resemble?' Renata tilted her head provocatively.

'A bird of paradise,' he returned promptly.

She preened herself. 'Very pretty.' She took a couple of steps and stopped. 'Give me your arm, please, these stones are crippling me!'

They proceeded back the way they had come, Alex and Renata arm in arm with Jan trailing behind, but when they reached the broad steps leading down into Harbour Street, Alex halted.

'Take my other arm, Jan,' he crooked it invitingly. 'You look as if you didn't belong to us.'

'Thank you, Mr Leandris, but goats don't need support.'

Alex laughed. 'Is that rankling?'

'Oh, don't be so touchy,' Renata scolded. 'Alex is only trying to be friendly, but you persist in snubbing him.'

'She's seeking to deflate my swollen ego,' Alex explained with a wicked grin.

'She's being stupid.' Renata was not sure what he meant.

'Oh, very well, just to show there's no ill feeling,' Jan slipped her arm through his, '. . . Alex.'

'That's much better,' he approved.

Bare skin touched bare skin, Alex's naked forearm and Jan's soft flesh. Again she had the sensation of an electric shock. The contact caused a vivid awareness to run through her whole body. It was almost shocking to discover that this man whom she was determined to dislike possessed a powerful physical magnetism which affected every quivering nerve. Was he affected too? She glanced at his profile, but his face was turned towards Renata and he seemed to be oblivious of her presence, so she decided he was not. But when having descended the steps she sought to withdraw her arm, deeming she had made her gesture, he clamped it close to his side. A natural reflex? His reaction towards prey which sought to escape? But it was not she he was trying to capture, and absorbed in Renata he had probably forgotten who she was.

'We must look ridiculous,' she protested, 'like the Three Musketeers or something!'

She made a more definite movement to free herself and he let her go.

'Renata is coming to have lunch with me on the *Artemis*,' he told her, naming his yacht. 'Will you join us?'

'Thank you, but no, I've work to do. If you'd drop me at the villa.'

'Jan is always so conscientious,' Renata observed.

Alex gave her a long, considering look.

'That's her trouble,' he said cryptically. 'But you and I, darling, are not overburdened in that way.'

Back at Kusadasi, Jan looked down at the graceful shape of the *Armetis* anchored in the bay. It made a charming picture with the small island with its sixteenth-century fort forming its background. She wondered if she had done the right thing, for alone on the yacht Alex would have ample opportunity to seduce Renata if so inclined. But if he were so inclined there would be plenty of others, and she would have suffered embarrassment feeling herself *de trop*. It might be he was going to propose and Renata would come back engaged. She wondered why such a satisfactory prospect left her feeling so cold.

CHAPTER THREE

RENATA did not come back engaged. Jan watched her closely, but she had neither the appearance of a satisfied lover nor of a prospective bride; she was moody, almost morose. Jan's anxious enquiries were met with irritable replies. She was perfectly well, she declared, but she was sick of Kusadasi, it was a one-horse little place and she wanted to go somewhere more lively. Alex might have found them accommodation in Izmir, which was more exciting. Jan thought he probably considered she would have too many other distractions there, but his courtship seemed to be hanging fire. He visited them most days, and entertained Renata and her father on his yacht, giving Jan perfunctory invitations to join them, which she always refused; he only included her out of politeness, and she had no wish to watch him flirting with her cousin.

Jeremy, in addition to the model he was going to make of ancient Ephesus, was writing a book about the history of the place, and Jan had plenty to do arranging his notes and typing his preliminary manuscript. Their stay was nearing its end. Jeremy had collected all the data and photographs he required for both projects, and drawn the designs for his model which was to be made at home. Denis Wood had gone back and Jan wondered if his departure had anything to do with Renata's dejection, since the situation between her and Alex remained unresolved.

The weather became hotter and dustier, and Jan found it debilitating. She became wan and was obviously wilting, but the only person who noticed her distress was Alex, Jeremy and Renata being too absorbed in their own interests.

'You should go home,' he told her, one morning when he was waiting for Renata. 'The climate evidently doesn't suit you. I assume you have a home?'

'Oh yes, my uncle's house is home and my aunt is there, but I can't leave Uncle Jeremy while he still needs me.'

'Much use you'll be if you collapse,' he growled, and for once neither voice nor expression was mocking, he seemed to be genuinely concerned, but Jan was determined to attribute the lowest of motives to all his actions; it helped to combat his growing fascination for her. He wanted her gone so that she could not intrude between him and her cousin, for if Renata was having qualms, Jan was her only support.

'I shan't collapse,' she declared, 'and I can't desert them.'

He shrugged his shoulders, and turned away, but his manner had been kind.

The air became more oppressive and Jan had the

sensation of waiting for a storm to break, both atmos-
pherically and metaphorically. Alex had given Renata
a beautiful cloak in silk brocade which she wore as a
dust coat. Its deep blues and greens flattered her
colouring and it seemed as if its long folds gave her
a feeling of security, as Moslem women still cling to
their concealing draperies in spite of emancipation. She
had never looked more lovely and Jan by contrast was
a pale little ghost, for though as tall as her cousin, she
seemed to shrink in the blinding sunshine. She began
to long for England's grey skies and green fields and
counted the days until their return. Storm clouds
gathered over the mountains of the interior, but they
never came any nearer and the sun continued to blaze
down on Kusadasi's white walls and red roofs, the blue
waters of the Mediterranean and the gleaming deck of
Alex's yacht, *Artemis*, anchored in the bay.

Then one evening the climax came.

Heavy cloud was rolling up from Anatolia and light-
ning glimmered from time to time. Jeremy had gone
out to visit a colleague and Jan stood at the window
watching the gathering storm hoping it would rain.
She had changed into a light dress for dinner and it
clung in its usual limp folds about her too-thin body.

'All in the dark?' It was Renata's voice and she
switched on the light as she came into the room. Jan,
who believed she was out, stared at her in surprise.
She was carrying her cloak and a suitcase, which she
dumped down upon the floor. Her beautiful eyes were
wild and scared.

'Jan, you must help me!'

'Of course I will.' Jan came to her and found she

was shaking. 'Darling, what's the matter? You're frightened.'

'Terrified.' Renata smiled wanly. She sat down upon the settee as if her legs wouldn't support her.

'But what's scared you?'

Renata glanced fearfully over her shoulder. 'Alex.'

'What on earth has the brute done to you?' Jan demanded wrathfully.

'Nothing yet, but I ... I can't go through with it.'

'Through with what?'

'You'll be shocked, Jan. I'm not good like you. I want all the lovely things he promised me, but now ... I can't!'

Jan perceived what was happening. The suitcase and cloak told their own tale.

'He's persuaded you to go away with him?' It was what she had feared all along, and her heart swelled with rage and indignation against Alex.

'Yes. He's leaving tonight and he ... he gave me an ultimatum. Either I must go with him or he won't see me again.' She twisted her fingers together and her big eyes were tragic. 'Once that yacht has sailed, I'll be utterly in his power.'

'You will,' Jan confirmed grimly, 'and apparently he's not mentioned marriage?'

'Oh, but he has ... when we get to Istanbul ... There'll be arrangements to make ...'

'Which he could have made here if he's in earnest,' Jan pointed out, not convinced Alex meant marriage. 'We've been here long enough.'

'That's just it. He says he won't be kept dangling any longer.'

Jan was surprised. 'You mean you're the one who's been holding back?'

'Well ... it was such an irrevocable step to take ... and there was Denis ...' Renata was not very explicit. She stood up and began to walk up and down the room. 'There's a storm brewing too, I'm sure to be seasick.'

'You mustn't go,' Jan said earnestly. 'You can't trust him, and he'll make you very unhappy.'

'That's what I'm trying to tell you. I can't go. I was mad to agree, but he promised me jewels, furs, anything I wanted, but I'd have to ... no, Jan, I can't. He terrifies me, I'm sure he's a brute in bed.'

Jan drew a deep breath of relief. So no harm had been done. Renata had not allowed herself to be seduced.

'Thank God you've come to your senses in time,' she declared. 'You'll tell him you've changed your mind?'

'That's it.' Renata glanced apprehensively at the yacht. 'I daren't tell him.'

'Oh, come off it, Rena,' Jan cried impatiently. 'Don't be such a coward. He's no right to persuade you to elope, if he's in earnest he should have come and asked Uncle in the proper way ...'

'Don't be so Victorian,' Renata cut in. 'A man doesn't ask Papa's permission to pay his addresses nowadays.' She laughed shrilly. 'Can you see Alex doing that? "Mr Reynolds, may I have leave to court your daughter?"' She sobered. 'Daddy's been part of the trouble. I've been afraid that if I turn Alex down, he might get the Turks to rescind Daddy's contract.'

'But surely Mr Leandris wouldn't be so petty?'

'Men can be spiteful when their vanity is wounded, and anyway Daddy is set on marriage between us.'

'But surely not if you're going to be unhappy? There's only one reason why you should marry Mr Leandris and that's if you love him. Then you'd condone his faults, and you wouldn't be scared, but apparently you don't, and if your motives are mercenary...'

'Oh, don't preach, Jan,' Renata interrupted. 'What do you know about love? Alex has a dark fascination for me, like ... like a snake's supposed to have. It's quite different from what I feel for Denis, that's a nice, matey affection. You can't imagine being fond of Alex.'

That, Jan felt, was true. Alex might inspire passion, even a turbulent devotion, but fondness did not apply. She could sympathise up to a point with Renata's apprehensions, Alex was not an easy person to gainsay, but to sacrifice her whole future because she was too weak to say no was quite preposterous. She said vehemently:

'You must stand up to him, Rena. He's no right to bully you into doing something that's not only foolish but wrong. You've no guarantee that he'll marry you when you get to Istanbul, in fact all this secrecy is very suspicious. Of course you mustn't dream of going with him, and if he comes here I'll tell him so.'

'Would you, Jan?' A gleam of amusement showed in Renata's eyes. The picture of Jan confronting Alex suggested a pekinese defying a wolfhound. 'But he wasn't coming here. I was to meet him on the quay where his dinghy will be waiting to take us aboard. I think he wants to avoid meeting you or Daddy.'

'Oh, does he? Then perhaps he has a little conscience after all. You won't go?'

'Then he'll come here to fetch me, and if I see him, I'll be lost.'

Jan sighed with exasperation.

'Look here, do you or do you not want to go with him?'

'Darling, I've been telling you, I just can't.' Renata's voice rose to a wail. 'You're so strong-minded. You don't know what it's like to be overruled, but I beg you, don't let me see Alex tonight.'

'If he comes, we'll lock him out.'

'That Turkish maid will let him in. She thinks he's a kind of god.' She looked round wildly. 'I must escape. Jan, help me!'

Jan realised her cousin was rapidly becoming hysterical. She could understand her panic up to a point. She had been playing with fire, and now the flame threatened to consume her, she was terrified of what she had done. But to be unable to put up any resistance against Alex's dominance struck her as amounting to feeble-mindedness. It was not as if he would use force ... but perhaps he might, being incensed by Renata's shilly-shallying. They were alone in the house except for the little maid who was no protection at all. She said sharply :

'Go and lock yourself in your room, Rena, and I'll go down to the quay to meet your ogre. If he won't accept that you're not coming, I'll call the police.'

She did not believe that the police would support her against anyone as influential as Alexandros Leandris, but he might be deterred by the threat of publicising his intentions. Renata jumped at her suggestion eagerly.

'Oh, would you, Jan? You're not afraid of him, I

know, and if anyone can persuade him that I don't want to come, it'll be you.' She giggled. 'Say some of the nasty things you've been saying to me, and you'll rout him.'

'I doubt it.' Jan did not quite like this description of herself as a sort of virago, but she was seething with anger against Alex. Hadn't he the perception to see that under her flirtatious manner, Renata was still innocent and he was doing her a great wrong by trying to abduct her, to say nothing of abusing her father's trust? Her initial low opinion of him was fully justified and she would have no hesitation in telling him just what she thought of him. Something of this she said to Renata, who gazed at her admiringly.

'You're wonderful, Jan. I wish I'd a fraction of your moral courage.' She looked at her wrist watch. 'But you must go now, he'll be waiting.' She glanced towards the window. 'The wind's blowing the dust about. Take my cloak, it'll give you some protection in that thin dress.'

'Thank you, Rena.' Jan allowed Renata to drape the garment over her shoulders, her mind already occupied with what she would say to Alex. 'Don't worry, Rena, I'll keep him out, and your father should be back soon.'

However much he favoured Alex's suit, Jeremy would never countenance the proposed elopement.

The short dusk was fading when Jan stepped on to the quay and the wind was blowing so that she wrapped Renata's cloak gratefully about her. *Artemis* was ablaze with lights, the reflections of which danced on the heaving waves. On the other side of the mole fishing boats and pleasure craft rode at anchor. For once there was

no cruise ship in port. Presently she discerned the
tender from *Artemis* moored to the landing stage, with
two of her sailors standing on the mole, identifiable
by their cap-bands, but there was no sign of Alex. Jan
looked at them doubtfully. She had expected to see
their master, but apparently he had not come ashore.
To beard him on board his own boat was more than
she had bargained for.

Catching sight of her hesitant figure, one of the men
came up to her.

'*Kalispera, thespoinis.*' He was Greek. He indicated
the boat. 'You come ... *né*?'

There seemed no option but to go if she wanted to
speak to Alex, and she smiled to herself as she pictured
his annoyance when he would have to delay to put her
ashore again. Clutching Renata's cloak about her, she
allowed herself to be helped down into the tender and
the craft shot out across the bay to the yacht. As it
came alongside, she saw that *Artemis* was a much bigger boat than it looked from the shore. Although
classed as a yacht, she did not carry sail and was driven
by powerful engines.

An iron ladder led to the main deck, and she was
assisted up it by the stalwart arm of the sailor who had
spoken to her; other seamen were gathered round the
opening in the rails to draw the boat aboard. Jan halted,
wondering how she could explain that it would be
needed to take her back again before being hoisted on
to its davits, but her guide propelled her forward towards the companionway.

'Mr Leandris ...' she began.

He nodded vigorously and pointed down a carpeted
stairway—no ladderlike steps for *Artemis*—and she

went down it marvelling at the luxury of the ship's appointments. She had never been on any sort of boat before, and had imagined the furnishings would be rudimentary, but that was not the case on Alex's super toy.

She was ushered into a sumptuous state room. A low divan covered with cushions was under the window, and it was a window, not a porthole, which was also the bed. There were tables and chairs, and sliding doors to a fitted wardrobe, another giving access to a private bathroom, the whole being decorated in gold and white. The concealed lighting threw a mellow glow over the decor. There was no sign of Alex, and after a moment's stupefaction she whirled round to demand his presence, but she was too late. The door had closed and there was the ominous click of a lock. She stared at its ornate panels aghast. Had Alex meant to abduct Renata, securing her so that she could not change her mind? It seemed like it. Running to the door, she beat upon it with her knuckles, but the cabin was soundproof. She stood biting her nails. This was something she had never contemplated. A movement of the ship increased her panic—it was casting off. Going to the window, she saw the quay receding, the lights of Kusadasi falling astern; *Artemis* had put to sea. Jan sank down upon the cushions on the divan, and then the funny side of the situation hit her and she giggled helplessly. Alex was going to have a disagreeable surprise when he came to find Renata. She was not afraid of him and the contemplation of his discomfiture gave her considerable satisfaction. It would serve him right for attempting to seduce her cousin.

Presently she stood up and went back to the window,

watching the sea glide by. The threatened storm had passed over, and the water was calm, the risen moon silvering the rippling swell, which here and there was agleam with phosphorescence. Once a dark shape leapt in the air, glittering drops cascading from its body, a dolphin at play, but still Alex did not come. She wondered whither the ship was bound—Istanbul, presumably. Alex would have to turn back when he discovered he had the wrong passenger. That would not please him. She gathered Renata's wrap about her, deriving an odd comfort from its clinging folds. The interview ahead would not be pleasant, but she was determined to tell Alexandros Leandris exactly what she thought of him. It occurred to her that Renata would have some difficulty in explaining her absence to her father when he returned, and he might radio the yacht if she admitted she was on it; but would she? She would not know for certain. Jan was more distressed to think of her uncle's anxiety than by her own predicament.

The key turned in the lock, and Jan stiffened as Alex came in. In the subdued light all he could see was a slender figure wrapped in Renata's familiar cloak. He looked magnificent, clad in a white mess jacket without tails, a frilled shirt, and a barbaric touch, a scarlet cummerbund bound about his slim waist, its fringed ends hanging down one side. His cat's eyes were aglow with anticipation, and Jan experienced a thrill that was neither fear nor repulsion. He really was a beautiful ... beast, and she could understand his fascination for her cousin. Tigers were beautiful too, and dangerous, and his were tiger's colours, black and gold.

'You will pardon this little formality,' he said pleasantly, as he relocked the door, but with a deep note in his voice which indicated he was moved by passion. 'My crew are curious and I did not want them to find an excuse to intrude upon you. Nor did I want to greet you under their watchful eyes. Ah, Renata, my treasure, at last you've come to me!'

A couple of strides brought him to her side, and he swept the concealing cloak from her shoulders. For a moment they stared at each other. Then he recoiled.

'You!'

Jan clasped her arms over her slight bosom.

'There's been a mistake, Mr Leandris ...'

'I should think there has! Where's Renata?'

'In Kusadasi. She sent me with a message from her. She'd changed her mind.'

A spate of profanity broke from his lips in a language which fortunately she could not understand. For a moment he was the primitive male deprived of his mate. His handsome features became convulsed with frustrated fury, and he clenched his hands; for a second she thought he might be going to strangle her. She went on hurriedly:

'I expected to meet you at the quayside to tell you Rena wasn't coming, and I had to see you personally, so I came aboard. I didn't expect to be ... confined before I could explain who I was.'

Alex had regained command of himself. His face was set and stern, as he said coldly:

'I suppose I have you to thank for this ... er ... intervention. You persuaded Renata not to come. The little fool must have told you where she was going.'

'She did, and she didn't need any persuading as she'd realised what she was doing. You acted very wrongly, Mr Leandris,' Jan spoke heatedly, and her eyes were full of reproach. 'Perhaps you've been misled by Rena's flighty ways, but she's a good girl, and you're a wicked man to try to seduce her.'

'Bourgeois morality,' he sneered. 'I could have given her everything she desired.'

'Except your name.'

He shrugged his shoulders. 'A permanent union would be a mistake since our backgrounds are alien. I thought she understood.'

'She's scared stiff of you,' Jan told him bluntly. 'You've intimidated her, Mr Leandris, and that's shameful. She came to me tonight and told me what you wanted her to do, and that she couldn't go through with it. She asked for my help. Since she was too frightened to come and tell you herself that she wasn't coming with you, I promised to bring her message. That's why I'm here.'

He did not appear to be listening, he stood glowering at her, and in spite of her bold front, Jan felt a twinge of fear. Renata had said he might be spiteful if his vanity was wounded, and her desertion had hit him hard. The beautiful stateroom, the lighted ship, his striking get-up were all to do her honour, and instead of the rapturous beauty eager for his embraces he had anticipated, he was faced by her insignificant self with her mouth full of reproaches. Almost she could feel sorry for him. She went on steadily:

'I'm extremely sorry to inconvenience you. If you'd met me on deck instead of this dramatic business of locking me in, I'd have explained at once, before you docked the dinghy. Now every minute is taking us further from the port, so if you'd kindly give orders to turn about ...'

'Turn about? What for?' he snapped.

'Why ... to put me ashore,' she faltered, not liking his expression. It had never occurred to her that he would not take her back, and surely he would not hesitate to do so.

'I'm very sorry,' she began hesitantly.

'You're not in the least, but before I've done with you you may be,' he told her ominously. 'That a shrimp like you should have the audacity ...' he broke off, biting his lip.

Grasping at her sinking courage, Jan reiterated:

'I repeat I'm very sorry to cause you inconvenience, but it's your own fault. If only you'd met me before you cast off, but now it's too late ...'

'Much too late. I've an appointment to keep tomorrow.'

'Oh dear!' She looked at him uncertainly. 'Can I ... get back from wherever it is you're going?'

'With difficulty.' He smiled unpleasantly. 'But I've a score to settle with you first. Don't pretend it isn't your influence that's kept Renata from me.'

'I don't. I've never approved of your behaviour towards her ...'

'Who the devil cares about your approval?' He was lashing himself into renewed fury. 'Between you, you and that vacillating cousin of yours have cheated me, made me look a fool—do you think I appreciate that?' His eyes were smouldering, and his voice sank, full of silky menace. 'Didn't it occur to you you might be taking a risk?'

'I expected you to behave like a gentleman, Mr Leandris.'

'You didn't. You labelled me chauvinist pig at our first meeting. Leopards ... and pigs ... don't change their spots.'

'I didn't like the way you were talking, Mr Leandris, and I don't care for the way you're speaking to me now,' Jan returned with spirit. 'I'd do anything for Rena, run any risk to help her.' Anger at his attitude overwhelmed her, her eyes sparkled and her slim body seemed to vibrate with the intensity of her feelings. 'You've behaved like a cad, Mr Leandris, trying to tempt her with all this sort of thing,' with one slim hand she indicated the cabin, 'to dazzle her with your wealth and good looks, but you've never won her love, which is the only thing that counts, you only overawed her. Thank God she drew back at the last moment. Why can't you stick to your bought women and leave innocent girls alone?'

'Because I didn't believe in Renata's innocence, and as you keep telling me, I'm a cad, and a pig.' He took a step towards her, with an evil glint in his eyes. 'I intend to live up to that reputation tonight.'

Jan backed away from him, moistening her dry lips with the tip of her tongue.

'What ... what do you mean, Mr Leandris?'

'You've defrauded me of my woman, but you're a woman too.' His eyes glittered. 'I need one tonight.'

This must be a nightmare, she thought wildly, it couldn't really be happening. Weakly she protested:

'You've never seen me as a woman before, you consider I'm plain and insignificant ...'

He interrupted: 'Presumably you've a woman's body

under that unspeakable dress, that's all that matters.'

Jan's face flamed. 'Good Lord, Mr Leandris, you're even more despicable than I thought!'

'Despicable, am I?' he snarled. 'I'll teach you to call me names!'

He seized her then, enclosing her in arms which felt like steel bands. He crushed her against his hard, lean body, and his mouth ravished her lips. Her first kiss ... only it was not a kiss, it was punishment for her presumption. She fought him desperately, but her puny strength was nothing against his, and deep down within her, something which she did not know existed stirred—the response of the female to a masterful male. She went limp in his arms and he dropped her down upon the divan. Instantly she was upon her feet again, and swinging back her arm struck him across the face with all her force, increased by her sense of outrage. He drew back with an oath, for Jan's slap had been hard.

'A wildcat, eh? It'll be a pleasure to tame you!'

'You're a brute!' she cried, hysterically, bewildered by the strange emotions surging through her.

'Brute, cad, pig—it gets monotonous.' He actually smiled. He touched the red mark on his cheek. 'You'll pay for this, my girl.'

Jan threw back her head, her small breasts heaving, her blue eyes wide and defiant. Her hair, loosened by the struggle, hung about her shoulders like a fine brown web. Her cheeks were flushed and she looked vividly alive, completely different from her usual colourless self. An appraising look came into the man's eyes; for the first time he was seeing her as a woman, and a woman with possibilities.

'I'm at your mercy,' she told him, 'but it's too much to expect you to be anything but ruthless. Do what you want to do, and I'll endure it, thanking God I've saved Rena from your clutches.'

Alex laughed. 'What melodrama!' he mocked her. 'So you'll endure my embraces because you can't avoid them.' The amusement deepened in his eyes. 'Perhaps I can teach you to enjoy them.'

His arrogant assurance enraged her.

'Never!' she cried furiously.

'Never is a long time.'

His manner changed, became curt and commanding. He went to the inset cupboard and extracted some diaphanous nightwear which he threw on to the divan.

'You will put that on and ...' he swept the cushions off it, 'and get into bed. When I return I shall expect you to be ready for me.'

'I'll do no such thing!'

He looked at her and there was something in his expression which caused her to quail in spite of her brave defiance.

'You would prefer that I strip you myself?'

'No, please, no!' She shrank away from him.

'Then do as you're bid. I'll return shortly.'

He went out, locking the door behind him.

Jan stood looking wildly round the cabin. She did not doubt he would do as he had threatened, and there was no escape. She went into the bathroom, but the bolt on the door was flimsy, Alex would soon force it. Then philosophically deciding she must accept her situation, she took off her soiled clothes and showered. The relief was exquisite. Reluctantly she put on the silken nightdress and negligee, and leaving her dis-

carded garments on the bathroom floor, went back into the cabin. She stood by the divan, gazing at it with
fast beating heart. Theoretically she knew the facts of
life, and she considered the sex act to be the final expression of love, and giving of body and soul to the
man who had won her heart, but there would be no
love about tonight's proceedings. A brutal deflowering
to assuage an angry frustration. She could expect no
gentleness from Alex, she could only hope it would be
quickly over, an unpleasant episode to be forgotten, if
she could, as soon as possible.

She heard the click of the key in the lock, and hastily
wriggled under the embroidered cover which disguised
the divan's true purpose. Beneath it were silk sheets
which were cold to her skin; she felt as if she had
turned to ice.

Alex came in. He had changed into a gorgeous
oriental robe in which he looked alien and sinister.
His black head was damp, as if he too had showered,
and the normally rigorously suppressed curls had
triumphantly asserted themselves, causing him to appear wholly Greek. She noticed then, her sharpened
senses aware of details, that his ears were slightly
pointed. A classical satyr, she thought wildly, and her
eyes went to his feet, half expecting to see hooves.
How could Renata have encouraged him? Not surprising she had turned chicken when it came to the crunch,
and she recalled with a shudder that her cousin had
said he would be a brute in bed. Now she must suffer
for Renata's folly.

Alex stepped lightly towards the divan. There was
no expression on his olive face, it seemed carved out of
marble. He stripped the cover off her and stood looking

down at her recumbent body. Defensively Jan had assumed the foetal position, her knees drawn up to her chin, her long hair covering her neck and chest, her face pressed into a cushion. She felt his hands upon her as he deliberately turned her over, straightening her limbs, and sweeping her hair back from her face and shoulders. His fingers moved over her, stroking her smooth skin lightly and caressingly. Their touch sent ecstatic thrills along her quivering nerves. His hands came to rest on her bosom, pressing her breasts gently, and she became aware of her own physical response. She could not endure much more of this, and keeping her eyes closed, she said through her teeth:

'Please hurry up and get it over.'

'What a charming invitation!' He laughed softly. 'Jan, Jan, you're more a woman than I thought, or you did either. When you've matured you'll be quite a girl.'

She made a convulsive movement, but his hands still held her down. She opened her eyes to find his face only inches from her own, his eyes full of amusement, his firm mouth curved almost tenderly. She had a wild impulse to raise her arms and fling them round his neck, to bring that imperious head down upon her breast, and she suppressed it with difficulty. Quivering, aware of dark forces rising within her, she waited for his next move, her body anticipating the weight of his.

To her surprise, he removed his hands and straightened himself, drawing the cover up over her as he said:

'You mayn't believe it, but I don't rape unwilling virgins.'

Astonished, she sat up abruptly, pushing back her hair.

'But you told me ...'

'That I would teach you a lesson. You've had it. I can imagine what went on in that prudish mind of yours while you were waiting for me. Now you may sleep in peace.'

The calm effrontery of his words stung her even through the tumult of her emotions.

'You're a sadist!' she accused him. 'Was it chivalrous to frighten a helpless girl?'

'Sadist?' he said musingly. 'That's a new one, but what else could you expect after provoking and challenging me? Be consistent, my dear. I was only living up to your opinion of me, and chivalry is scorned by the modern independent miss.'

Vaguely confused, she murmured his name, 'Oh, Alex ...'

He had turned towards the door and he swung round to look at her. Her wide, puzzled eyes met his with something in them with which he was familiar.

'Perhaps you weren't so unwilling after all,' he told her smiling. 'You underestimated me, didn't you? But even brutes and sadists have scruples. It would be poetic justice if you came to desire me, though that's a word you consider almost improper, don't you?'

'That's impossible!' she cried feverishly, fearing he might be speaking the truth. This strange new yearning which filled her being must be desire, the need of a woman for a man. But she did not want Alex, she could not. He was ... what was he? She stared at him blankly, wondering if all the labels she had attached to him could be wrong. She did not really know him at all, she had only judged him by his behaviour to Renata, who, she had to admit, had led him on, and his arrogant manner. Her breasts still tingled from the pressure of his hands, her body was protesting that she had been denied what she desired, but desire was not love. She could never love Alex, and this belated rousing of her senses brought her down to his level. She was bewildered and shocked.

'I'd be more likely to fall for the devil,' she declared emphatically.

'His Satanic Majesty has a fascination all his own,' Alex returned imperturbably. 'And I've been compared to him more than once, but never forget you're on the side of the angels, so I must be anathema to you.'

Jan had drawn up her knees and clasped them with her bare arms. She sat regarding him with a sort of wistful wonder, her eyes contradicting her caustic tongue. The subdued lighting made her flesh appear translucent and gave mystery to her long eyes. It found threads of gold amidst her light brown hair. She looked very young, vulnerable and appealing. Alex passed his hand across his brow with an impatient gesture.

'Don't look at me like that, girl,' he said harshly, 'or I may change my mind. Goodnight, Jan.'

He went out, closing the door firmly behind him.

CHAPTER FOUR

JAN lay awake after Alex had left her, trying to calm her agitation and take stock of her situation. Apparently Alex was bound for some unnamed port from which he would presumably send her back to Kusadasi, though he had not sounded very co-operative about that, and she had no money and no passport, but he could not want to prolong her stay upon his ship, and she did not believe he was quite such a heel as to abandon her. Besides, surely her uncle would make some enquiries about her when she failed to return to the villa. Presumably when she was missed Renata would tell her father where she had gone, but neither of them would expect her to be on the yacht. Mercifully they were not the worrying sort, but they might imagine she had fallen off the quay. If they went to the police, she hoped it would mean trouble for Alex, for he had behaved abominably. What excuse he could offer to Jeremy for abducting her she could not imagine, that it was in mistake for his daughter would hardly placate him, but Alex was inventive enough to find a plausible reason.

She must insist that he do something next day to allay their anxiety, for she was too spent to tackle him tonight, even if she knew where to find his quarters aboard. That she would have to face him in the morning, unless he intended to keep her locked up, was not a pleasant prospect, for he had outraged and insulted her, though he had spared her the ultimate degradation. Her body was sore from the violence of his first embrace, but with self-disgust, the recollection of it caused a retrospective excitement to stir in her veins. She had never in all her short life been so stimulated and alive as she had felt during her exchanges with him, but he was vindictive and cruel, and it was all the more galling to have to admit he could so affect her. But she was not afraid of him, she told herself feverishly; he had might on his side, but she had cunning. She had won the first round at slight cost to herself, for she had saved Renata, and now Alex's initial anger was spent she would be in no physical danger from him, for he could not possibly find her desirable.

The motion of the ship was soothing, and at length her nerves quietened and she was lulled into sleep.

Jan awoke to find the sun pouring in at the window, and a woman, presumably a stewardess, offering her a cup of tea.

'Kalimera,' she said, and she had no English, for when Jan asked her what time it was she shook her head. But she had a message to communicate, for after cogitating for a while, she came out with, 'Petit déjeuner,' and pointing to the ceiling, 'Deck,' from which Jan gathered breakfast was to be obtained up above, and she was anxious to demand that Alex reassured her relatives.

She showered, and, wrapped in a big towel, hunted for her clothes, but there was no sign of them. She stood biting her lips, for she could not go up on deck arrayed only in a bath towel, and she was hungry, having missed her dinner the night before. The tantalising smell of coffee drifted in through the window which the woman had opened, increasing her appetite.

There was a bell beside the divan and she pressed it hopefully. Almost immediately the stewardess returned, and Jan indicated by signs that she wanted her clothing.

'*Né, thespoinis,*' the woman said; she was far from being a girl, with a pleasant but by no means handsome face. Evidently Alex did not seek amorous entertainment among his staff. She opened a drawer and presented Jan with a clean set of nylon underwear, and took from the cupboard in the wall a silk dress which she offered to her with a beaming smile. Jan wondered if Alex kept a stock of garments for his stray females he enticed on board, but she could not possibly wear them. She shook her head and tried in English and her schoolgirl French to explain that she wanted her own things.

The woman got the message, and with elaborate pantomime and the inflections of her voice, made Jan understand that the dress she had been wearing was soiled and unsuitable for yachting. She made rubbing and wringing gestures to indicate that Jan's clothes were being washed, all but Renata's cloak, but over that she shook her head.

'Sun,' she said, pointing outside. It was not the right wear for a bright, hot morning.

Reluctantly Jan dressed herself in the borrowed plumes, realising that if she did not she would get no breakfast. The dress was white with a navy blue stripe down one side and along the hem. With it went a little blue silk jacket with short sleeves. It fitted fairly well and it certainly looked nautical. Jan did her hair in its customary knot in her nape, and went on deck.

Breakfast was laid under an awning in the stern—coffee, crisp rolls, butter, honey and a big bowl of fresh fruit, including the ripe figs for which Turkey was famous. Alex was waiting for her seated in an upright canvas chair, and there was another opposite to him. He was all in white, trousers, deck shoes and a short-sleeved singlet with a striped V neck. In spite of her resentment against him, Jan's heart leaped when she saw him, he looked so handsome and debonair. They both said good morning formally, and he sprang up to arrange her chair.

'I see Ariadne found you something to wear,' he remarked as she seated herself a little selfconsciously. 'We keep a spare wardrobe for guests who get wet through or lose their luggage. You look very fetching, except for your hair. Why will you wear it in that unbecoming style?'

'Because it's neat and tidy,' she returned, as he resumed his seat. 'I've thought of having it cut short, but then I'd have to keep having it trimmed. But my hairstyle can't be of interest to you.'

'Why not, since I have to look at it?'

'Unfortunate, isn't it?' She gave him a gamine grin. 'Your sailors' zeal is responsible for that. They shouldn't have been in such a hurry to get me aboard.'

'Oh, I don't know.' He leaned back in his seat. 'I find the present situation piquant. Shall I pour your coffee?'

'Thank you. Well, I find the situation deplorable. You must do something to let Uncle Jeremy know I'm safe.'

'That has already been covered by radio. I'll ring him from Istanbul with full explanations.'

So he had not been too incensed to allay her uncle's anxiety. She gave him a grateful smile.

'What possible explanation can you give?' she asked.

'Easy. I'll tell him I've borrowed you to do some clerical work for my mother, her own secretary having been taken ill, and we hadn't time to inform him as he was absent and I had to leave in a hurry.'

Jan wrinkled her brows; she thought it sounded a bit thin, but Jeremy was so vague he might swallow it.

'So you have a mother?' She was curious about the lady.

'Yes, she lives in Istanbul. Why do you look surprised? Most men have mothers. I had a father too, but he died prematurely of a stroke through overwork.'

There was nothing remarkable about Alex having a parent, but somehow she had never connected him with a family.

'Do you live with her?' she asked.

'I stay with her when I'm in Istanbul. She has a charming house on the Bosphorus. You'd like it.'

'I daresay, but I shan't see it. As soon as we reach land I must go back to Kusadasi.'

'How?'

Just the one word, with a glint in his eyes. Jan suppressed a sudden qualm and said severely:

'That's your problem. Since you've carried me off, it's up to you to get me back again.'

'We'll reach Lesbos in about an hour,' he told her. 'I'm meeting a colleague at Mithimna. He is on his way to Rhodes, so it seemed a convenient rendezvous. Our business is confidential and private, so we chose this out-of-the-way spot. Then I shall proceed to Istanbul. You'll have to accompany me.'

'Meaning it would be difficult to find transport from Lesbos?'

'Precisely.'

Jan digested this. It seemed she must spend several days aboard the *Artemis*.

'I'm afraid I'm an unwelcome guest,' she said diffidently.

'Not at all,' he returned gallantly. 'I find your society quite diverting.'

'In spite of my hair-do?' she asked provocatively, while she quelled her rising alarm. She did not want to provide a diversion if it meant any more scenes like the previous night.

'That can be remedied,' he grinned. Then he became serious. 'It would be a waste of time for you to return to Kusadasi, for as you know, your visit is nearly at an end. I suggested to your uncle that he might like to spend a few days in Istanbul on his way home, as he wants to see the Ephesian relics in the museum and the pillars taken from the temple in St Sophia, but evidently he hadn't got round to relaying the suggestion. He and Renata can collect you on their way home from there.'

So he had plans to contact Renata again, and had not relinquished his pursuit of her. Jan broke a roll with a vicious gesture as if she wished it were his head.

'I shouldn't think Rena would come.'

'Oh, she will,' he asserted confidently. 'If only to discover how I've taken her desertion.'

'If she's any sense . . .' Jan began.

'She hasn't.' Alex's eyes slid appreciatively over

her slight figure. She ate daintily, and her fingers and wrists were delicately formed; her long throat was graceful and well set upon her shoulders. She was fine-boned and thin-skinned, though men never noticed her in detail when Renata was around. Alex was observing her now with the eye of a connoisseur, and evidently liking what he saw. 'She may find she's been superseded,' he added.

'Probably.' Jan never dreamed he could possibly be thinking of herself. 'I imagine you've a host of female admirers to console you.'

'You sound as if you thought I kept a harem.'

'Isn't that rather to be expected ... in Istanbul?'

'My dear girl, those days are long past. Most Turks have only the means to keep one wife, without indulging in concubines, and the law decrees monogamy.'

'Hard luck.' Jan was trying to needle him. She was finding his intent scrutiny disconcerting. No doubt he was comparing her unfavourably with her cousin, who should have been sitting in her place if his plans had not gone awry. 'But there's no law against mistresses, is there?'

'Only moral disapproval.'

'Which I don't suppose troubles you.'

'Again, my dear, you're drawing naïve conclusions about situations of which you're ignorant.'

Her eyes flashed up to meet his tawny gaze and she saw irony in it. The word naïve annoyed her.

'I shan't be so ignorant if I see much more of you,' she said with deliberate provocation.

'If you're alluding to last night, I can and will repeat the treatment if you continue to be impertinent.'

Against her will she blushed furiously and her heart

knocked against her ribs. He looked so cool and calm
this morning she had forgotten his demeanour concealed a sleeping tiger. There was a gleam in his eyes
which warned her he might mean what he said. She
blurted out:

'But you can't enjoy embracing a plain jane like me.'

'Which again betrays your ignorance ... or innocence. You're not really plain, I see great possibilities
in you. If you'd let my mother take you in hand, she'd
transform you.'

'Thank you very much, but I don't want to be trans-
formed!'

'Liar—you'd give your ears to put that flamboyant
cousin of yours in the shade.'

Jan laughed merrily. 'I've never been jealous of
Rena's looks. I admire her too much, and you must be
feeling piqued to descend to such gross flattery. I
know my limitations only too well.'

She began to peel a peach, but her blue eyes were
wistful. If only she had a chance to detach Alex from
Renata ... What was she thinking about? She loathed
the man, didn't she? The last thing she wanted was to
attract him. He had shown what a brute he was last
night, and yet ... she looked at his well shaped hands
and brown muscular arms as he started to light a
cigarette, and to her horror felt a surge of desire to
feel them around her again, the firm mouth drawing on
the cigarette crushing her lips. What was happening
to her? She had never had such sensual thoughts before, but then she had never met anyone like Alex
to arouse them. She pushed aside her plate and rose to
her feet.

'If it's all the same to you, Mr Leandris, I'd like to take a walk along the deck.'

He looked up at her with inscrutable cat's eyes and she hoped fervently he had no inkling of what was in her mind. She kept her own eyes downcast, and her long lashes made shadows on her cheeks. She did not know it, but she looked innocently alluring.

'By all means, but don't fall overboard. Your virtue is in no danger, so there's no need to have recourse to extreme measures.'

'I never thought of such a thing.'

'No? But you might. Strange notions seem to seethe in that well shaped head of yours.' Of course he was laughing at her, and she looked at him scornfully. 'But since we're together in rather intimate circumstances ... through no fault of yours, of course ... don't you think you might call me Alex? At least for the voyage?'

Jan's heart sank. The voyage—how long was she going to be cooped up with this unpredictable man? She looked round at the blue sea, noticing the humped shape of one of the innumerable Aegean islands on the horizon, and up at the blue sky—no storm clouds about this morning—and again at the handsome man lounging in his chair. Suddenly she experienced a complete reversal of feeling. Why shouldn't she enjoy this adventure which had so fortuitously come her way? The yacht was luxurious, the scenery lovely, and Alex ... well, he was stimulating company.

'Very well, Alex it shall be ... for the voyage,' she said demurely.

'Good.' He stood up. 'Will you allow me to show you over the ship?'

'With pleasure ... Alex.'

They moved off side by side. He was playing the charming host, his antagonism apparently forgotten. She said bluntly:

'Am I forgiven for interfering?'

He gave her a sidelong narrow look, but did not answer her question. Instead he observed:

'Since we've been thrown together for a few days I see no point in existing in a state of war. Do you?'

'I'm quite ready to accept a truce.'

'Are you now? You're being magnanimous, Miss Reynolds,' he mocked her. 'I suppose when you're secure in the bosom of your family, you'll open fire again?'

'That depends upon how you treat Rena.'

'Oh, bother Renata. She isn't here, and you are.'

Recalling the previous night, she said firmly: 'But not as her substitute.'

'My dear girl, you could never be that.'

'Of course I can't, though you seemed to have had a different idea last night.'

Alex looked very faintly ashamed.

'If we're to preserve our truce, you'd better forget about last night.'

They had reached the stern and leaned over the rail to watch the widening V of wake following the ship's passage.

'That is quite impossible,' Jan retorted with vehemence. 'You made an indelible impression, but I'll not refer to it again.'

She saw a flicker of amusement cross his face and wished her last words unsaid. They could be taken as a compliment, which was not what she had intended. But it was only too true, that night was burned into her memory for all time, all the more so because she was unlikely to ever again feel such emotions. She eyed him surreptitiously as they turned and walked back along the other side of the deck. What a beautiful creature he was, but how unpredictable. Now he seemed anxious to win her approbation, and eliminate her first impressions of him, but she must not allow herself to be deceived. Beneath his suave exertion he was as ruthless and domineering as he had ever been. Yet though she wanted to despise him she was unwillingly drawn to him by his personal magnetism. An expression she had read somewhere recurred to her. 'An enchantment of the senses.' That was what he was doing to her, enchaining her senses, aided by the luxurious appointments of his yacht, but such sensations were wholly ephemeral, she did know that much; only the very young mistook them for something much stronger.

They went all over the ship, and it was a beautiful boat. There was a lounge and saloon, both done in the prevailing white and gold. There were other guest cabins, but he did not show her his own. On the bridge she was intrigued by the various instruments used in modern navigation, especially the asdic which showed neighbouring shipping like black fish in a green sea.

Then Alex left her in a deck chair to doze in the sun, and being tired after her restless night, she fell asleep.

When she awoke, the ship was at anchor, and Lesbos lay ahead of them, an island of green and brown slopes, with a castle crowning the hill above the little town of Mithimna. Jan stared at it trying to recollect where she was and what had happened. Then as remembrance returned, Alex came towards her dressed for going ashore in a conventional white suit. Again he seemed to have changed, he was every inch the business executive from his smooth head to his polished shoes, complete with briefcase under his arm.

'I'm afraid I must leave you until after lunch,' he told her politely. 'Your meal will be served in the saloon.'

She looked wistfully at the island.

'Can't I go ashore?'

'Not now,' he said firmly.

'You mean you don't want to advertise my presence on your yacht?'

He shrugged his shoulders. 'I couldn't care less, but I'd rather you didn't go unescorted. I'll come back for you later on. We might have dinner at the hotel. You'd like that?'

'I would,' she said eagerly.

'Well, be a good girl, and we'll do that.'

He left in the yacht's tender, for there was only a small harbour. Jan stood at the rail watching the boat diminish in size as it approached the shore. She became aware of another ship in the vicinity also at anchor. That must be Alex's colleague's vessel. She wondered vaguely what business intrigue was afoot to necessitate a secret meeting. The water rippled against the sides of the ship. Relieved of their master's presence, the sailors were singing. Presently she was summoned to lunch, which was served to her ceremoniously in the white and gold saloon. The steward eyed her curiously when he thought she was not looking, and she smiled to herself. He must be wondering what had induced his master to take aboard such an ordinary piece of goods. Even her clothes were borrowed. That turned her mind towards the night's entertainment. Wasn't Alex delaying their arrival in Istanbul by lingering on the island, when his business was concluded? She could hardly credit he was doing it for her sake, there must be some other attraction of a more frivolous nature of which he had not informed her. The thought was depressing; she did not want to be an unwanted third at his dinner party. She decided she would tell him she had changed her mind about going ashore.

In the afternoon, Ariadne brought her laundered clothes to her cabin, and she changed the blue and white silk for her own cotton dress. It seemed even less becoming and she surveyed herself in the bathroom mirror with distaste. Well, that was she, Janet Reynolds, in her ordinary guise, and if Alex disapproved it was just too bad.

Alex did. He returned when the sky was aflame with the sunset, with the sleek satisfied air of a man who had concluded a satisfactory deal. The other ship was preparing to depart.

She met him as he stepped aboard.

'Well, that's concluded,' he said cheerfully, 'and as I wished. Now I think I deserve a little relaxation. Missed me?'

'It was rather dull without you,' she conceded. 'Alex, I don't want to go ashore, I've changed my mind.'

'But you were so keen, and I've ordered dinner.'

She fell back on the well worn feminine excuse.

'I've nothing to wear.'

'Rubbish, there's a whole wardrobe full of clothes in your cabin. There must be something that will suit you.'

'Thank you, but I don't care to wear other women's dresses,' she said stiffly.

'They don't belong to any other woman, they're *pro bono publico* . . .'

'I don't know what that means, and I prefer to wear my own clothes.'

'As represented by that limp rag?' He seemed to recollect himself. 'Doubtless it's very suitable for . . . er . . . your daily tasks, but not for dining in a hotel. There'll be a dinner gown in the cupboard.'

'There may be a dozen, and I'm staying aboard.'

'No, my dear, you're not.' He spoke almost gently and taking her by the arm, led her out of earshot of the grinning sailors, who although they did not understand what was said, guessed a disagreement was in progress. His use of an endearment startled her and his touch wrought havoc along her nerves.

'Don't be a little idiot, Jan,' he went on. 'Those dresses are no more than fancy clothes provided for emergencies, like you find yourself in now, a piece of foresight on my mother's part. She often sails with me and after a gruelling afternoon I'm in the mood for light entertainment. It'll be no fun to dine alone, and I'd be grateful for your company; but you wouldn't feel comfortable in what you've got on,' his voice became coaxing, 'so let Ariadne maid you and come along. I'm going to change myself.'

So there would be no other woman, and Jan capitulated. She very much wanted to go ashore, and only her pride and independence had prompted her to refuse him. She had been so sure that the wardrobe had been discarded by one of his lady friends, but it appeared that was not so and she was spiting herself by her obstinacy. She very much wanted to appear glamorous before Alex, if she could.

Ariadne was more than helpful. They chose a green dress with a chiffon overlay, the flowing lines of which did much to disguise Jan's angularity. It was a little large, but a wide sash bound it round her slim wist. The low neck was trimmed with diamanté. The Greek woman did her hair for her, piling it up on top of her head and securing it classical fashion with two silver bands so that the graceful line of her neck and shoulders was exposed. Jan stared at her unfamiliar reflection in the glass with surprise.

'Why, I'm really quite good-looking!' she exclaimed.

Ariadne did not understand her words, but she was pleased with her handiwork and smirked complacently. Jan went to join Alex with renewed confidence. Wherever they were going he would have no cause to feel ashamed of her, she was thankful that she had allowed herself to be overruled over the dress. He was garbed as he had been on the previous evening, and the sight of him so clad brought back a flood of recollection that caused her a moment's unreasoning panic, but his expression held no threat, he was smiling benignly. He exclaimed when he saw her :

'The cygnet has become a swan!'

'You mean the ugly duckling. I suppose I did look like one. Surprising what a difference clothes can make, but I'm the same me underneath.'

'I hope so, I rather like that me.'

She dimpled. 'That's a change, but it amuses you to tease me, doesn't it?' Her eyes clouded. 'You find me awfully naïve.'

'I find you quite charming.'

She shot him a nervous look. She distrusted his compliments.

'You have a silken tongue,' she remarked, 'but you needn't waste it on me. I prefer sincerity.'

'Why don't you think I am sincere?' he asked, taking her arm to guide her down the companionway.

'Because I can see you make a habit of buttering women up. It oils the wheels, doesn't it? Except of course when you're angry.'

'You'd be improved if you applied a bit of butter yourself,' he retorted. 'You're more likely to get your own way if you use a bit of flattery, most men are vain.'

'Thanks for the advice. I'll remember it.'

He conducted her to an emergency door in the bowels of the ship, which meant that they could step straight out into the tender without exposing their finery to the hazards of a ladder. The sea was as smooth as a pane of glass under a star-spangled sky. The lights of the little town were reflected in the dark water and the castle on the hill above it was floodlit.

They dined out of doors in an arbour under a trellised vine, at a hotel situated a little way up the slope to the town. They ate stuffed avocados, shellfish soufflé and spiced lamb. Jan had ice cream for dessert and Alex the local goats milk cheese. He ordered Muscat for her to drink, observing he did not suppose she liked resinated wine, in which he was correct. He seemed well known there, the staff served him swiftly and efficiently, and he addressed them all by name. There were other guests, but they were unobtrusive; in their leafy bower they seemed to be alone. Alex talked about the islands, and their stormy history. Greek, Italian, Roman and Ottoman had swayed their destinies until finally they became Greek. When they reached the coffee stage, the proprietress herself came to speak to them, a big dark woman who spoke English. Alex introduced her as Leda, and she seemed to know him well.

Studying Jan critically, she asked: 'The *thespoinis* is your betrothed?'

'No, my concubine,' Alex promptly replied.

Jan did not even blush, as she suspected he had hoped. She was becoming used to his peculiar humour, but she was about to protest until she saw the mischief in his eyes and that Leda did not believe him.

'It is time that you wed, *kyrie*,' the Greek woman said. 'You need a son to follow you, but this little one is too thin and pale. Leave her with me for a month and I will fatten her, make her strong, to be the mother of fine sons.'

She was called away to the telephone, and Alex enquired: 'Does that programme appeal to you?'

'Certainly not! I'm not a brood mare,' Jan declared indignantly. 'Your lady friend has most primitive ideas.'

'The islanders' ideas are fundamental,' Alex told her. 'They consider a woman's prime duty is to produce a male child, and that is her fulfilment. Until she does she's negligible.'

'How elemental,' Jan scoffed, but she was thinking it might be a wonderful achievement to bear Alex's son. Anxious that he should not divine her thought, she went on hurriedly: 'I'd be obliged if you'd show more consideration for my good name. Calling me your concubine, indeed!'

'You lost that when you came aboard my boat,' he returned drily.

'Oh no, no one would think ...' she was going to

say no one would believe she could attract Alex, but she knew how malicious gossip could be. 'No one will know,' she concluded lamely, 'unless your friend talks.'

'Leda? She is the soul of discretion, she has to be in her trade.'

At that point Leda returned. 'Another cruise party tomorrow,' she said, with a sigh, 'but it is good business. *Kyrie*, before you go will you have a word with Stephanos? He likes to see you.'

'Certainly.' Alex rose. 'Please excuse me,' he said to Jan.

'Ah, but the *thespoinis* must come too,' the woman said, and laid her hand on Jan's arm. Alex seemed about to protest, then shrugged and followed them into a room in the hotel, entering by a french window. A teenage boy lay on a couch, with beautiful dark eyes and the same classic profile as Leda's, obviously her son. His face lit up when he saw Alex, and he sat down beside him, speaking to him in Greek. Leda drew Jan aside.

'My son was very ill, he needed a very expensive operation. Kyrios Leandris sent him to Athens and paid many drachmae for his treatment. Now he will recover. We bless the *kyrios*' name.'

Alex looked at them suspiciously. 'What are you whispering about, Leda?'

'Nothing, *kyrie*, but you like to hide your light under a bushel,' Leda declared.

Alex laughed vexedly. 'Since you've gone all Biblical, isn't there a text about not letting your left hand know what your right hand does?' He glanced at his watch. 'It is getting late, we must be getting back.'

They took their leave and crossed to the yacht in

silence. Jan was digesting this new aspect of Alexandros Leandris. Obviously Leda and her son adored him and he had gone out of his way to help Stephanos. Since she had assessed him as selfish and unfeeling, it was disconcerting to discover a more human side to him. She wanted to believe he was a cad and a reprobate, it was her defence against him, and to find he was otherwise was too dangerous. When they had re-boarded the ship, she said to him:

'It seems you like to keep your good deeds under cover.'

'If you're referring to Stephanos, what if I did do the kid a good turn? A few drachmae means nothing to me, that doesn't make me a model character. Don't go running away with the idea that I'm a do-gooder or you'll be sadly disillusioned.'

There was an edge to his voice and she recalled that he had not wanted her to accompany him to see the boy and discover what he had done.

'Well, if you'd prefer that I should continue to think you're a callous brute . . .' she began uncertainly.

'I'd much prefer it,' he cut in. 'It's nearer the truth.'

'The hard, bitter cynic?' she gibed.

They reached the door of her cabin, and he stepped in front of her so she could not enter it.

'Exactly, and I'll prove it. Did you enjoy your evening?'

'Very much, and thank you.' She looked up at him uneasily; he was looking very formidable.

'Then wouldn't you like to express your thanks appropriately?'

She froze. Surely he couldn't mean . . .?

'I . . . what do you want?' she stammered.

'Oh, not to share your bed,' he said lightly. 'But a kiss wouldn't cost you much.'

He was so near, almost touching her, and in every nerve she was conscious of him. Her body ached for his embrace. Closing her eyes, she raised her face, murmuring breathlessly :

'Then take it.'

'Oh no, if I were going to take I wouldn't ask. I want you to give it.'

A quiver ran through her, but she made no move, some sort of paralysis constrained her limbs. She wanted to, but she couldn't.

Alex waited while tension built up between them, then he shrugged his shoulders.

'Evidently you're not feeling generous. Goodnight.'

He came away from the door, after pushing it open for her to enter, then he strode away without a backward look.

Jan slowly entered her cabin in a welter of self-reproach. Why could she not do as he had asked? A kiss meant nothing. But that was just it. To him it would have been merely a graceful way of saying thank you. He had kissed Leda when they left the hotel, lightly and carelessly, and he had expected a similar action from her. But she was not in the habit of bestowing casual kisses, and for her it had much greater significance. It meant capitulation to the beast, acceptance of his attitude towards Renata. She was sure that he automatically sought to subjugate every woman who came within his orbit, even so humble a person as herself, but until he made clear his intentions towards her cousin, he was still her enemy. When they reached

Istanbul their truce would end. Regret returned to self-congratulation that she had been strong enough to refuse him.

CHAPTER FIVE

THE *Artemis* sailed in the small hours, and when Jan awoke, it was to see land upon either side as the yacht entered the Dardanelles. Her sleep had been haunted by troubled dreams of Alex. Through various obstacles, mist, flood and even fire, she was trying to reach him with an important message, but always he eluded her. When finally she thought she had come up with him, pushing her way through briars, she found no human being, but a snarling tiger. That part was all too vivid, and she woke in a cold sweat, with her hair all about her face, which accounted for the briars. She lay for a while reflecting upon the inconsequence of dreams. Her subconscious must have identified Alex with the beast to which she had sometimes likened him, but he had not been at all tigerish on the previous evening. Ariadne arrived with her morning cup of tea, and a pile of laundry. Not only had her own clothes been washed, but also the ones she had worn the day before. After she had bathed, she looked with some distaste at her dowdy cotton frock, then yielded to temptation and put on the navy and white silk. It was much more becoming than her own dress, and she did not want to shame Alex in front of his crew, she told herself, though she knew the excuse was flimsy. She wrestled with her hair, trying to do it as Ariadne had done, but her efforts were a failure; it was too fine and soft to be easily manipulated. Finally she plaited it, made the plaits into a door-knocker in her nape, but left it loosened about her face, tying a flimsy scarf over her head. There were plenty of those in the cabin wardrobe.

When she came on deck she found Alex was break-fasting with the captain. This gentleman was officially in charge of the yacht unless Alex chose to take command. He was a short, thickset man with a roving eye. Both men stood up when they saw her, as she stood hesitating, and Alex waved to her to come forward. The captain brightened visibly as his master introduced them. His name was quite unpronounceable. He left them after an exchange of platitudes, and Alex became preoccupied while she ate her rolls and fruit. He had papers beside him to which he kept referring. Thus she had plenty of opportunity to study him. In repose his face was a little sad, the well shaped mouth firm but not hard. Long black eyelashes veiled his eyes. He was younger than she had first supposed, there were no lines on his smooth face, the hands which held the papers were long-fingered, beautifully formed and sensitive. She wondered about him. He must be hard-headed and ruthless to hold the position he did, at his age, and she could sense his force and drive. Women, she surmised, were only a relaxation to him, and if he did marry Renata it would be because she would do him credit, a decorative addition to his household; she could not imagine him in love. Passion he had in plenty, she had experienced some of that, but no softer feelings.

He looked up and caught her speculative expression,

and instantly his eyes became full of mockery.

'Well, have you come to any conclusion?'

She blushed. 'You're an enigma, Mr Leandris.'

'Alex, please, and I thought it was women who are supposed to be mysterious, though I've never found them so. I'm just a plain hard-working business man, with an eye for a pretty girl. What I want I take, if I can get it, but so do most people. And now you must excuse me, I've work to do in connection with yesterday's deal.' He collected his papers.

Jan offered to type for him, but was told brusquely that no typing was required.

'You'd prefer the role of secretary to concubine?' he enquired as he rose to go to his cabin, with a mischievous glint in his eyes.

'Definitely.'

'I wonder.'

'You needn't. The one's my trade, the other ...' She shook her head. 'Apart from the moral issues I've no amatory arts, you'd find me disappointing.'

He gave her a long, level look which caused her colour to rise.

'You still don't know your potential, Jan,' he told her, and with that cryptic utterance he left her.

Jan went to the rail to watch the flow of traffic as the yacht entered the Sea of Marmara, and there was plenty to see—cruise liners, battered merchantmen, caiques, ferry boats and dozens of smaller craft. Some of the bigger ships lay at anchor, waiting for a pilot. Jan wondered if Alex would have dared to withdraw if Renata had been aboard. Her lovely cousin would not accept neglect, but she herself would rather be without his company, she told herself mendaciously, for she missed his stimulating presence, especially during lunch, which she was served in solitary state in the saloon; the master, she was told, begged to be excused, he was having a sandwich in his stateroom, and was hard at work.

They did not reach Istanbul that day. The *Artemis* anchored off one of the islands in that sea, and Alex remained incommunicado until dinner, by which time Jan was heartily tired of her own society. There were books in the lounge, but she was too restless and apprehensive to read. She did not know what Alex intended to do with her when they reached port. Apparently dump her on his mother, a prospect which was vaguely alarming. No landing party went ashore, the yacht lay still in a calm sea. Almost she could wish a storm would arise, and there were sudden squalls in that locality, but nothing happened, and dusk gathered softly over the quiet water. Jan did not change for dinner, and neither did Alex, but she had to discard her scarf, and she unplaited her hair, letting it flow loose over her shoulders. As she had secretly hoped it attracted Alex's attention.

'Forgive this informality,' he apologised as he came into the saloon where she was waiting for him, 'I'm too tired to dress up.' And he did look weary after his hours of concentration. 'I see you haven't either, and I like the hair. It really is quite lovely.' He walked up to her, lifting up a strand of it between his finger and thumb. 'And fine as silk.' His eyes narrowed as he dropped it. 'Your possibilities are endless, my dear.'

'I'm not your dear,' she retorted, moving away, for his nearness affected her strongly. 'And my possibilities, though I'm not sure what you mean by that, are nothing to do with you.'

'Now, now,' he protested, as they seated themselves. 'What about our truce?'

'That doesn't necessitate insincere endearments.'

'More prickles!' He gave a mock sigh. 'What do you want to talk about? The history of ancient Byzantium? Believe me, personalities, however insincere, would be much more entertaining.'

'No doubt, but history is a much safer topic.'

'Ah!' His eyes gleamed. 'You consider I'm dangerous?'

'That's why I'm here. You thoroughly put the wind up poor Rena, and I think you *are* a danger ... to her.'

He gave her a quizzical look, and addressed himself to the very excellent fish soup the steward then placed before him. Naturally he employed a good chef and the food was always delicious.

After that he did embark upon Byzantine history, partly because the man kept coming in and out and showed himself to be very knowledgeable.

'The city was eventually conquered by the Turks,' he concluded. 'The sultans at the Topkapi palace were a cruel vicious lot.'

'And kept vast harems?' Jan queried curiously.

'Oh, of course.' He leaned back in his chair. The food had revived him and he was his usual derisive self. They had reached the dessert stage, and Jan was eating rum baba, soaked in spirit and topped with cream. 'Women were less important than cattle, and treated worse. Did you know that when a new odalisque was summoned to the sultan's bed, she had to enter it from the bottom and work her way up past the imperial feet ... quite a feat, forgive the bad pun.'

'No, I didn't know. You seem to be quite an authority on seraglios. Do you regret not possessing one yourself?'

His face expressed sheer horror.

'God forbid! Imagine having a dozen lovely ladies all clamouring for the honour of sharing one's bed.'

'You'd be equal to it,' she retorted, 'and of course you'd select the one you liked best.'

'Don't you believe it! There was protocol in the seraglio. The reigning favourite exerted considerable influence, even in politics, although she was never seen in public. No, Jan, a plethora of jealous women would not appeal to me, and besides ...' He gave her one of his wicked looks.

'Besides what?' Jan asked innocently.

'It isn't the most beautiful women who are best in bed.'

Jan looked at her plate. 'You should know,' she said non-committally, wondering what had prompted that remark. Deciding the conversation had gone far enough upon that subject, she reverted to Turkey's role in the Great War and the rise of Mustapha Kemal.

'A great soldier,' Alex commented, 'though he was a bitter enemy to Greece. Do you know what he considered to be the essential quality in his women, and he was no ascetic.'

She shook her head.

'Availability,' Alex informed her drily.

Jan hastily sought another topic. Where were these ambiguous remarks tending? Was he expecting her to become available in Renata's absence? Surely she had indicated plainly that she would never be that? Though he might charm and intrigue her she would never so forget herself. But, as she had told him, he puzzled her. If he really wanted her, there was nothing to stop him. She was wholly within his power and she feared he could soon break down her resistance if he tried. She was considerably more vulnerable than upon the night of her arrival, for her hate and loathing were fading away. But of course he did not. He was only amusing himself by teasing and baiting her until Renata arrived, and he liked to see her blush. That facility was becoming less frequent as she became accustomed to his innuendoes. But the amusement for that evening seemed to have palled, for after coffee he left her, saying he needed a good night's rest.

The *Artemis* docked next morning below the Galata Bridge. Jan was up early on deck to watch their approach. A mist lay over the Bosphorus, out of which the domes and minarets of the mosques seemed to float in the sky. It was a city of magic.

Over breakfast Alex told her he must leave her to go to his place of business to report on his deal.

'You'll have to stay on board as you haven't a passport,' he told her. 'I hope your uncle remembers to bring it.' Then seeing the disappointment in her face, 'Oh well, perhaps I can wangle a landing card. The Turks are a bit lax, they probably won't even look at it, not like our neighbours on the Black Sea. Have you any money?'

Jan shook her head. 'I didn't come prepared . . .'

'Naturally.' He threw a fat purse on the table. 'There's English and Turkish money in it. Don't get lost, and if you do get into any difficulty, take a taxi back to the yacht. There are plenty to be had. Mind you're back before dark.'

She picked up the purse. 'Of course I'll repay ...'

'Oh, of course, and maybe I shan't ask for cash.' Again the wicked gleam in his tawny eyes, but Jan did not rise, it was merely Alex's nonsense again. 'Be a good girl and keep with the tourists if you can,' he went on, 'and look out for pickpockets.' He surveyed her critically. 'You won't appeal to the Turks, they like their women plump, in fact, fat, so I don't think you'll get abducted. Buy yourself a hat. I'll see the Captain about your card, get it from him.'

He went striding away down the deck. A while later Jan saw him running lightly down the gangway on to the quay, dressed in his formal white suit with his brief-case under his arm. He did not look up, evidently he had completely dismissed her from his mind. Jan fingered the purse he had given her, marvelling at his changes of mood. He pretended to be so hardbaked and indifferent to her feelings, taking every opportunity to taunt her, yet, knowing she was longing to go ashore and explore, he had made it possible, absorbed as he was in his own concerns. She thought regretfully how much she would have liked him to accompany her, but that was too much to expect—and then she chided herself fiercely. He was nothing to her at all, and she could enjoy herself much better freed from his teasing presence.

Jan did spend a very enjoyable day, wandering round the old part of the town, 'doing' the mosques and the Topkapi Palace. She bought herself another of the white linen hats most of the tourists were wearing. Since she appeared modest and inconspicuous, no one attempted to accost her. She even ventured into a European-looking café for lunch, and resisted the temptation to buy souvenirs in the great glittering bazaar. The money in her handbag was not her own.

Dutifully, as the sky began to blaze with the sunset, she returned to the ship, walking over the Galata Bridge, with the Golden Horn on its further side, as crowded with vehicles as the water below it was packed with craft. Lights were beginning to appear and the sky behind the minarets was red-gold, orange and mauve. There was no mist tonight.

Alex returned for dinner and told her he had booked accommodation at the Hilton for her relatives, who would be arriving next day, flying from Ankara.

'But you, Miss Janet Reynolds, must stay with my mother,' he concluded.

'But why?' She did not at all want to lodge with a lady who, if she resembled her son, would be formidable. 'I'd much rather stay with my own people.'

'Because, my prickly pear, we must preserve the fiction that I engaged you to act as secretary to my mother ... for Jeremy's sake. He, as you know, would be upset if he learned the truth. Fortunately he's so vague he won't realise how improbable our story is.'

His tone was entirely matter-of-fact, without a hint of shame or regret for his part in the attempted elopement with Renata. He had not shown any compunction for the outraged father's feelings if he had succeeded. Jan wondered how he had intended to placate him.

'But what'll your mother think?' she enquired.

'Oh, she'll play along with us when I've explained the situation,' he said easily, and Jan conjectured unhappily what that explanation would be. She recalled having been told that Mrs Leandris was English, though she never associated Alex with his British blood, he always seemed so foreign, but it was reassuring to realise that her hostess would be a countrywoman.

'She *is* English?' she asked, desiring confirmation.

'Yes. In fact I'm a bit of a mongrel,' he told her. 'My Turkish grandmother gave up her country and her family to save my Greek father from the Turkish army who were looting Izmir—Smyrna it was called then. They escaped together in a small boat and reached Lesbos, where they were married. That is what I call true love, to sacrifice everything for a man. *She* didn't bother about her feminine rights. She gave herself entirely into his hands.'

'Well, since she was a Turk, she'd expect to do that,' Jan commented. 'But it's a romantic story,' she went on hurriedly as she saw him frown, 'though I'm surprised you appreciate it. Were they happy?'

She asked the question eagerly, for the sequel to this mating of enemies seemed important to her. Greek and Turk had been at each other's throats and each had a different culture. If they could compromise so could ... others.

'Ideally. My father was an only son. There were several girls, all of whom married Greeks. Zillah Hanim was, I'm told, always completely subservient to her husband. It made for a harmonious married life.'

'Indeed?' Jan's blue eyes sparkled irefully. 'Of course you would approve of that. Like the unfortunate Victorian wives, she was practically her husband's slave.'

'Don't you believe it, spitfire. A clever woman can always get her own way if she's subtle enough. Victorian women weren't fools and a lot of them ruled their households and their husbands without appearing to do so.'

'You won't find Rena is acquiescent,' Jan declared. 'She won't descend to diplomacy to get her way. She'll expect to be given it.'

Alex threw her a quizzical look.

'You're assuming that I intend to marry your cousin?' he enquired silkily.

'You must be, since you've arranged for her to come here.' She eyed him doubtfully, his smooth olive face was blank, but there was a mischievous glint in his eyes. 'I hope this time you're going to act honourably, Mr Leandris.'

'Isn't that rather a lot to expect of a chauvinist pig and—let me see, what were the other things you called me?'

Jan flushed, she had hoped he had forgotten them.

'I know you better now,' she said steadily. 'And I don't believe you're as bad as you try to make out.'

'Then don't rush to the other extreme and whitewash me,' he warned her. 'I keep telling you, I'm not a paragon. As for Renata, I thought you said she was terrified of me and that's why she sent you with her message.'

'She must have got over her fear if she's ready to come here and meet you again,' Jan pointed out, for she too had found Renata's actions inconsistent, but she had found her own explanation. 'She panicked because she sudddenly realised the irregularity of her position if she went with you. She would have been entirely at your discretion, and the thought frightened her.' Jan's blue eyes hardened. 'I'll never forgive you for leading her astray.'

'But nothing came of it, and if I repair my error and offer her marriage, you'll forgive me?'

'I suppose so, I don't bear grudges.' She turned her head away, for although now it seemed inevitable, the thought of Alex's union with Renata was painful to her, and not on her cousin's account. It was absurd it should be so, for she was not in the running at all, nor did she wish to be, she assured herself angrily. Alex was not and never could be the sort of man she would want to marry.

Alex was studying her averted profile with a curious expression, as he asked:

'You're certain she'll accept me?'

'Of course. It's what she wants, to be your wife. That Greek woman said you needed one.'

'Yes, I'll need to come to it in the end.' He smiled ruefully. 'And I think I've found the right woman.'

It was too much to expect that he would admit to being in love. Jan was doubtful if he were capable of love as she understood it, but she knew her standards were high. Renata would be content with lip service if her material needs were satisfied.

'Yes, you've done that,' she agreed. 'Rena is so beautiful, and she is virtuous, though you doubted it. Of course she has no dowry, which I believe is expected in your country, but you're rich enough not to consider that, and you know she attracts you.'

'Does she?'

Jan made an impatient movement. 'Don't pretend. You wouldn't have courted her so assiduously if she didn't.'

'Perhaps I wished to ascertain her ... limitations.'

Jan looked at him severely. 'You're being perverse.

If, as you say, you've found the right woman, it must be she. You haven't looked at anyone else for weeks.'

'Conclusive evidence,' he smiled sardonically. 'It's the first time I've heard a woman plead another woman's cause.'

'Which goes to show what a selfish lot you mix with. Rena is very dear to me and I'd do a lot to make her happy.'

'What makes you so sure that marriage with me would make her happy?' Alex asked gently.

Jan looked uncomfortable, for if she were honest, she must admit that Renata was strongly influenced by what Alex could give her. That she was coming to Istanbul would indicate that she was anxious to resume relations with him, and she had recovered from her momentary panic. To Jan's innocent mind that could only mean that her cousin had discovered that she could not do without him, or so she sought to convince herself.

'Rena isn't independent like I am,' she said, avoiding a direct reply to his question. 'She needs a strong man to ...' she checked herself, about to say, 'keep her in order,' and changed it to, 'direct her. You and she will make an ideal couple.'

And in looks they certainly would.

'You think so?' Alex was bland.

'Anyone can see that,' Jan declared. 'And your having sent for her and her father proves you must have had a change of heart. Uncle Jeremy would never countenance a ... a liaison, and Istanbul's your home town. You'll be taking her to see your mother, won't you, and after that ... I suppose your engagement will be announced.'

'Your interpretation of my motives is masterly,' Alex told her, and she was too intent upon her theme to notice the irony in his voice. 'Renata would be a bride of whom any man might be proud. She would look magnificent at the head of my table, decked out in the jewels she'll expect me to give her.' Jan glanced at him quickly, but he was smiling urbanely with a sensual glow in his cat's eyes, which encouraged her. He was envisioning Renata in all her splendour and the image pleased him.

'But you?' he went on in a changed voice. 'What'll you be doing when I and Renata are canoodling in nuptial bliss by the Bosphorus?'

'I'll go back to England, what else should I do?' Suddenly the prospect seemed utterly bleak. 'I intend to get a full-time job, with I hope a good salary, and be independent of everybody.'

'You make a god of independence. You'd consider it ignominious to be supported by a husband?'

'Not at all. A good marriage is a partnership, I'd do my share looking after the house and children.' Jan moved uneasily under his penetrating gaze. 'But I'm unlikely to get married, so I must make my own life.'

'I'm glad you don't despise matrimony.'

'Of course I don't,' she declared a little impatiently. 'But we were talking about Rena. I don't count.'

He gave her a veiled look, seemed about to say something, and changed his mind. Jan watched him anxiously, he seemed to be moving in the right direction but she was still unsure of his intentions.

'What a loyal little champion you are,' he remarked, 'your cousin should be grateful to you, but I doubt if she will be. She won't appreciate our sojourn together.'

'She's not so petty,' Jan declared heatedly. 'She'll know it couldn't be helped.'

'I hope you can convince her of that.' He regarded her keenly. 'Just how well do you know Renata?'

'A lot better than you do. We were brought up together like sisters and we'll always stand by each other.'

'All right. Granted Renata is an angel of light and I'm ... the opposite, but knowing all you do of me I'm surprised you're so ready to trust your precious cousin to me.'

'I believe you could make her happy if you tried,' Jan said simply. 'You've been very good to me after ... after the beginning, and then of course you were terribly frustrated.' Alex grinned at this naïve excuse. 'I'm sorry for all the nasty things I've said to you. You don't deserve them.'

'Coals of fire,' he drawled, 'or is this feminine guile to push me in the direction you want me to go?'

'You know very well nobody could ever push you around,' Jan retorted tartly. Her voice became appealing. 'You do want Rena, don't you?'

'How could I not do so, so beautiful and desirable!' Again the ironic note, and this time Jan noticed it.

'You won't let her down?'

'I always fulfil expectations where your sex is concerned,' he returned blandly. 'Except upon one memorable occasion when they were more fearful than pleasurable.'

Jan blushed and hung her head, and he stood up.

'But that's enough of your delightful cousin for tonight. She isn't due until tomorrow and you'll make me ill with anticipation if you go on about her.' Irony had given place to mockery, the cat's eyes were taunting. 'Come up on deck and see the city lights, they're quite a spectacle.'

They stood together at the stern in what seemed to be a fairy world. Lights glittered everywhere, from the buildings along the Golden Horn to Uskudor across the straits, reflected in the dark water. The walls of Topkapi Palace and several of the mosques were flood-lit. Ferry boats illuminated from stem to stern moved over the dark depths like gilded comets. Cruise ships dressed all over with coloured lights lay at anchor along the quays and above them were the great white stars which seemed bigger and brighter than in Western skies.

Entranced, Jan gazed at it all, until she became aware that Alex had moved. He stood in front of her, a hand on either side of her imprisoning her against the rails.

'Am I still to be denied that kiss, my prickly pear?'

Her heart began to thump. He was a head taller than she, and she dared not raise her eyes above the level of his white shirt.

'Rena . . .' she stammered.

'Is still far away. The crew are all down below. There's no one but you and I alone amid light and stars. No, they can't see us——' as she glanced to-wards the passing ships, the traffic-laden bridge, 'they're too far off. Tomorrow you'll be well chaper-oned in my mother's house, and you said, perhaps mis-takenly, that I had been good to you.'

His voice was low and coaxing and though he had her there, helpless before him, he made no move to take her. He wanted her to give, and it was not much he was asking. Every callow youth expected a kiss after an evening's entertainment, and Alex had given her much more than that. The only surprise was that he should want her to kiss him. She supposed vaguely that it was because she had so often criticised and provoked him. He wanted to assert his mastery over her, but if it would give him any satisfaction, she would not continue to deny him. He had called her ungenerous and that Jan was not; moreover, she felt no repugnance, her senses were clamouring for his reciprocation. It was because of that that she was hesitating. She feared she might betray too much of the emotion he awoke in her. With an effort, she raised her arms and clasped his neck and standing on tiptoe, brushed his cheek with her lips.

Alex laughed. 'Oh, come, Jan, you can do better than that.'

'I need ... some help,' she faltered.

'What a confession!'

His arms closed round her, drawing her away from the rail. He held her gently but firmly, looking down into her shadowed face with an inscrutable expression. Jan felt a flood of feeling surge through her. With a half sob she pressed herself against him. His arms tightened with sudden crushing force, and his lips came down on hers, fierce and demanding.

Jan lost all sense of place, time and even of identity. She clung to him, giving him back kiss for kiss, her whole body aflame with the intensity of her passion. She seemed to have no bones, her slight form moulded into his lean strength. This was ecstasy and pain, but the pain was part of the rapture. She longed to be made part of him, their union complete. When she had reached a point when she could bear no more without the relief of consummation, though she was unaware of the true nature of her need, his hold slackened and

he withdrew his face from hers. He supported her to
a low bench set by the entrance to the companionway
and let her sink down upon it. She was trembling and
she covered her face with her hands with a low moan
of frustration.

'Very nice, Jan.' His voice was faintly mocking. 'But
you've had all that's good for you, unless . . .'

'Unless . . . what?' she murmured, hardly knowing
what she was saying, longing for a repetition of his
kisses.

'We continue the session in your cabin.'

That reached her with the impact of an icy shower.

'No!' she gasped.

'I feared that was too much to expect,' he drawled.

'You said you didn't rape virgins.'

'Unwilling ones,' he corrected her, 'and it wouldn't
be rape.'

For a moment she was tempted. To lie all night in
Alex's arms . . . but no . . . he would only be contemptuous of her surrender. Another woman who was unable
to resist him. Besides, he was pledged to her beautiful
cousin and when Renata appeared on the morrow he
would abandon her to claim the more glamorous girl.
She surmised, and was probably correct, that it was the
hunt that excited him and once the prey was in his
clutches he lost interest. He had taken this opportunity
to subdue her and if she surrendered he would not give
her another thought, nor would he bestow any more
of his attentions upon her once Renata had arrived, but
she would have preserved her integrity. With an im-
mense effort she controlled her unruly emotions and
managed to say calmly :

'You've no cause to call me ungenerous now, Mr

Leandris, but as you said, we've gone far enough. I hope you're satisfied.'

'Satisfied!' It was almost a groan.

'Oh, Alex,' she cried piteously, 'don't make me hate myself!'

He said in a changed voice:

'I would loathe to do that. Forgive my importunity, Jan. As you're always telling me, I'm a selfish beast. You'd better go below now and get some rest, you've had a long day.' He added as she hesitated: 'You're quite safe from me.'

'Yes, I know that,' she returned almost mechanically. The danger was not from him but from within herself. 'Goodnight, Alex—and thanks for everything.'

'You've nothing to thank me for,' he said roughly. 'I only please myself.'

She rose a little unsteadily to her feet, and drew the front of her dress together where his impatient fingers had torn it.

'Not always,' she told him gravely. 'Just now . . . you forbore.'

Both knew that if he had persisted she would have given in to him.

But now he had become his usual derisive self.

'Still determined to fit me with a halo?' he jeered. 'Perhaps the temptation was not great enough.'

Perverse being, consistently denying his better self. He meant to wound her, but oddly enough, self-deprecating as she was, she was not hurt. Instinct more accurate than reason assured her his desire had been genuine and he had conquered it out of deference to her wishes.

'Goodnight, Alex,' she repeated gently.

He did not respond, but as she went down the companionway he stood at the top of it watching her descent with an expression that was neither derisive nor contemptuous, it was almost tender. But Jan did not look back.

CHAPTER SIX

JAN lay awake for most of the night. Through the windows of her cabin, for it was hot and she had opened them wide, the noise of the traffic was a background for her troubled thoughts. Lights flashed across them from passing craft and the occasional blare of a siren mingled with the general cacaphony.

She had to face the realisation that she was in love with Alexandros Leandris, and the knowledge offended both her pride and her fastidiousness. She was recalling with vivid clarity his words before he left her on that unforgettable night, that it would be poetic justice if she came to desire what she had rejected. It had appealed to his perverse humour to seek to bring that about. Their dinner on Lesbos, their conversations with their erotic undercurrent had all been aimed at that object. Sure of his invincibility, he had deliberately sought to rouse her ... and he had succeeded. For him it had been an amusing diversion to relieve the tedium of the voyage, for her disaster, for she could never take love lightly as he did, though in his case it was not love at all.

Jan vowed to herself that she must never, never allow him to learn how he had triumphed; that would be

too humiliating, for she knew he had only been playing a game with her, and had no genuine regard for her
at all. If she were hurt, he would consider it was her
just deserts for taking Renata's place.

The incident on deck that night had caused her to
betray herself, but she could minimise that by pretend-
ing she had been playing along with him for kicks ...
the 'fun' so many girls indulged in, in their search for
sensation. She smiled wryly. She had certainly gained
some new sensations, but she was ashamed of them,
for even if they had been prompted by love, they were
not reciprocated, and she must not let Alex suspect
how deep the experience had gone with her. She could
not bear the thought that he might tell Renata and
they would laugh together about poor lovelorn Jan's
pitiable condition.

Heartless though he might be, she did not believe
he would have come to her bed on the eve of his reconciliation with Renata.

That had merely been a try-on to discover if she
were ripe for surrender, and if she had been acquiescent
he would have teased her about her change of heart. He
had always insisted that he was no saint and had
laughed when she had sought to endow him with more
worthy attributes. She had thought she had discovered
a kindlier, more human side to him, which for some
obscure reason he concealed beneath his mask of pride
and arrogance. At times they had seemed to be almost
en rapport, and there must be some sort of physical
affinity between them, as he could not embrace her if
she were wholly repulsive to him, but that was not
much comfort, for it could only be some kind of
chemical reaction which prompted his amorous ad-

vances and won her response. To him Janet Reynolds had been a provocation and a challenge, and that night he had known that she was ready to be seduced if he had pressed her, it had been his final triumph.

She should scorn him for his callous exploitation of her feelings, but she could not do so, for she had wanted him and she still did. Every nerve in her body ached with longing for his arms and his lips and that humiliated her. It had seemed impossible she could ever come to love such a man, but no other word could describe this yearning she felt towards him, and it was all the more painful because she had given her heart to an unworthy object.

Yet was he so unworthy? In the business world he had no equal for drive and ability. He could be magnanimous, as was shown by his generosity to Stephanos, who reverenced him as a man as well as a benefactor. He had been generous also to herself after the initial conflict, though he had every reason to resent her. It was only with regard to women that his conduct was questionable, and upon that subject she was very ignorant with only her old-fashioned standards to guide her. Renata had often told her that her ideas culled from books were out of date in a permissive world. He was a superior person and she need not be ashamed of loving him, but she must keep her feelings concealed if she did not want to earn his mockery.

Her present position was a far from happy one. She was to be foisted upon Mrs Leandris, who could hardly be expected to welcome her, in support of a fiction concocted for her uncle's benefit, while Alex went off to greet Renata with the intention of asking her to be his wife. She would have to congratulate them and endure her cousin's smug complacency, for Renata would believe that her evasive tactics had brought about the desired result. Jan could only hope that her ordeal would be short and she could escape within a few days to England where she could lick her wounds in private, for here she must maintain a pretence of indifference, and nobody in Istanbul would give a damn for her feelings.

The morning found her pale with dark-circled eyes, and after a little hesitation, she dressed in the blue and white outfit. She felt she could not face Mrs Leandris in one of her shapeless cotton dresses. She would return it as soon as she had access to her travellers' cheques and could buy something becoming, for her luggage would have been brought from Kusadasi. Her sojourn with Alex had made her conscious of her sartorial shortcomings and she would have a better chance of securing good employment if she looked more prepossessing.

It took all her resolution to go up on deck to meet Alex for breakfast instead of staying in her cabin. She hoped he would not allude to the previous night, and there was something she must impress upon him if she were to avoid Renata's ridicule, and since she was no actress it would not be easy to make herself convincing.

Alex's good morning was perfunctory and his manner absent, as he perused some papers beside his plate. He was wearing a formal suit in pale grey, with blue tie and socks, and the unfamiliar garb changed his appearance. This was Alexandros Leandris, the business magnate, with his mind occupied with more important matters than personal affairs. The meal was consumed in silence. Jan had no appetite, though she drank several cups of coffee and played with some fruit. With her eyes on the distant domes and minarets she was wondering how to approach the subject that filled her mind.

Alex suddenly looked up from his papers, fixed her with a penetrating glance, and said abruptly:

'You had a bad night?'

She started and flushed. 'The quay was a little noisy,' she offered as an excuse.

'Indeed?' His mouth curved in a wicked smile. 'Had you allowed me to come with you, you would not have been conscious of outside distractions and when you did sleep it would have been the deep slumber of exhaustion.'

Jan's colour deepened at this evocative statement. Alex was in one of his worst moods of provocative teasing, but he had given her the opportunity to put on her act.

'You always treat matters of the heart with levity, don't you, Mr Leandris? As for last night, you gave yourself a field day, trying to find out how far I'd progressed under your tutelage.'

She tried to speak flippantly, and concealed the fact that her hands were trembling by clasping them in her lap.

He frowned at her heavily.

'What are you trying to say, Jan?'

She shrugged her shoulders. 'I didn't take you seriously, of course. I never have. It was a chance to discover what this love business is all about.'

Was she talking nonsense, or would he get her message?

He smiled wryly.

'You'd have learned more if you'd carried the ... er ... experiment to its logical conclusion.'

She shook her head, essaying a brittle laugh.

'Oh no, that was going a little too far. I draw the line at the bedroom, or in this case, the cabin door.' She drew a deep breath and went on, preserving with difficulty her tone of light raillery. 'We've had quite a lot of fun on this trip one way and another, haven't we, Alex? I must thank you for being so amusing. But that's all it's been, a bit of fun.'

He stared at her for so long that Jan found it difficult to maintain her airy pose. Then he said:

'I didn't think you were the kind of girl who appreciated amorous play.'

'Ah, but as you've said, I didn't know my own potential. I've changed a bit since I came aboard your yacht. I don't think I'll make a habit of flirtation, it might become boring with repetition.'

'You're talking a load of rubbish,' he said shortly.

'Am I? It's you who've taught me to appreciate ... rubbish. And that's all it was last night.' She quoted solemnly, 'Most friendship is feigning, most loving mere folly.'

'I fail to see what all this is in aid of.'

'Oh, I thought you might be afraid you'd broken my heart. But my heart wasn't involved. That's what I'm trying to say.'

The tawny eyes met the blue ones and Jan tried to smile archly. His expression was inscrutable.

'I understand,' he told her, and returned to his papers.

Jan realised that she need not have been afraid that he would mention her to Renata. He had already dismissed her from his mind; she was not important enough even to be a joke. Self-preservation required that she should convince him that her indifference equalled his, and apparently she had succeeded, but she felt no satisfaction, only an infinite regret. He glanced at his watch and collected his correspondence.

'If I'm not to be late at the airport, we must be going. I'll drop you at my mother's first. Ariadne has provided you with a suitcase. It will look more respectable to arrive with some luggage.'

There was a gibe in his voice and Jan felt a moment's panic. What was his mother going to make of her unconventional escapade? The suitcase would accommodate Renata's cloak and her dress, she had nothing else to pack. That reminded her of what she was wearing.

'I ... I'll return what I've got on to you when I've bought something else,' she said hesitantly. 'But I thought you'd like me to look my best to meet your mother. The dress I came aboard in was a bit tacky.'

'Hardly your best when you're bog-eyed with frustration,' he said brutally. 'Oh, keep that garment, you've earned it.'

'Thank you for it and your consideration,' she returned with a touch of sarcasm. 'But you're going to have a lot of explaining to do, Mr Leandris.'

He shrugged his shoulders. 'Never explain and never apologise,' he told her, 'it saves a lot of trouble. I notice we're on formal terms again ... Miss Reynolds.'

'Your mother won't expect us to be ... intimate.'

'What, after spending three days in my sole company?' His eyes glinted. 'My mother knows me better than that. Ah, here is Ariadne with the case, and we'd better hurry.'

The Greek woman approached them across the deck, carrying a small case which she handed to Alex, saying something to him in her own language. He nodded, taking it from her, and turned to Jan. 'Are you ready, or do you want to powder your nose?'

He looked at her nose as if he considered it needed some attention, but Jan shook her head.

'I'm quite ready, Mr Leandris,' she said tonelessly.

As they walked along the quay, Jan turned to look back at the *Artemis*. She was preparing to leave her berth to seek her permanent mooring. Her superstructure was white against the blue sky, the Greek flag hung limp from her stern in the windless air. For Jan she had been the locale of the most harrowing scenes in her short life, and some moments of pure bliss, but she would never board her again.

Lydia Leandris was not at all what Jan had expected. She had anticipated a tall, stately personage with Alex's colouring, instead of which she was confronted by a small, fair woman with the remnants of a pink and white prettiness, and her eyes were as blue as Jan's.

Her house was charming, a white villa on the shores of the Bosphorus, with a wide terrace in front of it looking over the water, furnished with garden chairs and marble urns of potted plants. It was rather noisy, as not only did the coast road run by it, it was on a slight eminence, but the seaway was thronged with ships which always seemed to be blaring sirens for some reason or other.

Visible from it was the Europe to Asia bridge, which

was Turkey's pride; tall enough to permit liners to pass beneath it, it was the much-neeeded link between two continents.

They were expected, as Alex had phoned his mother, and a little Turkish maid ushered them into a dim cool room scattered with oriental knick-knacks, venetian blinds drawn to exclude the sun.

It was obvious Lydia adored her son. She ran to meet him as he came into the room, her face alight, and threw herself into his arms.

'Well, wanderer, am I to have the pleasure of your company for a while?' she demanded, after they had kissed, 'and . . .' catching sight of Jan, 'is this the girl?'

Her eyes ran over Jan's slight form with a puzzled frown. She was not at all her son's usual type.

'Yes, I'm staying for a while,' Alex replied, 'and Miss Reynolds is your new secretary.'

'But I told you I didn't need a secretary. Maria gives me what help I need with my small correspondence.' She looked at Alex severely. 'What have you been up to, you bad boy?'

'Oh, Jan'll explain,' he said carelessly. 'I can't stop now, I've some friends to meet, but I'll be in for dinner. Meanwhile please make J . . . Miss Reynolds . . . welcome. She's had a rough time.'

Jan stepped hastily between him and the door, feeling he was deserting her.

'I think you should wait to inform Mrs Leandris . . .'

'I haven't time, and you'll do it much better than I should,' he returned blandly, brushing her aside. He turned back to say : 'Tell her everything.'

The door closed upon his exit, he had, as he had told her, evaded explanation or apology. If she was to tell the whole story, she would not spare him, and if it did not reflect well upon him, that was his fault, he should have stayed to give his version.

'Sit down,' Lydia Leandris said gently. 'I'll tell the maid to bring some coffee. Then you can tell me what that wicked lad of mine has been doing.'

Evidently she did know her son very well.

Left alone, Jan glanced round the gracious room, with its light furnishings and marble floor covered with Chinese rugs. The colour scheme was blue and cream, the settee upon which she had seated herself being of carved white-painted wood with a blue-upholstered seat. There were crystal vases of roses here and there. The whole effect was bright and airy. So this was Alex's home, when he was at home, which apparently was not often. Would he expect Renata to live with his mother? She did not think her cousin would agree to that.

Lydia returned with the maid carrying the coffee tray which she placed on a low table. She seated herself in a chair opposite to Jan. She wore a well-cut linen jacket and skirt, and had the air of a conventional British matron, but her years in a foreign country had broadened her mind. While the coffee percolated, Jan told her story, omitting only the incident upon the night of her arrival on the *Artemis* and trying to gloss over Alex's original intentions towards Renata.

'My cousin is very romantic,' she said untruthfully. 'They had planned an ... elopement, but at the last moment Rena got cold feet.' And she hoped she sounded convincing.

'She was rather foolish to trust Alex so implicitly,' Lydia remarked. 'My son is no better nor worse than

the average man, nor has he much use for romance.'
She started to pour out the coffee. 'Milk and sugar,
Miss ... er ...?'

'Yes, please, and do call me Jan, you see Rena is also
Miss Reynolds and it can become confusing.' Jan rose
to take her cup.

'Very well, Jan. So you think Alex intends to marry
this cousin of yours?'

'Haven't I made that plain?' Jan seated herself again.

'You've tried too,' Lydia's wry smile was reminiscent
of her son. 'Many girls have hoped to capture him, but
he's played about long enough. It's time he settled
down.' She stirred her coffee meditatively in its delicate
china cup. 'A wife and family would steady him, and
at his age, over thirty, he should be getting himself
an heir. So far none of the girls who've attracted him
were able to hold him long enough to get engaged,
and of course, in this country, men expect a dowry.'

'Is that obligatory?' Jan asked anxiously, for she
knew her uncle had little to spare to dower his
daughter. He would consider her beauty sufficient recompense for any man.

'No, but it's customary.'

'Well, I think it's an absurd custom,' Jan told her
in her downright fashion. 'Alex ... I mean Mr Leandris has more than enough for a dozen wives. I'm sure
he won't expect one.'

Lydia raised her arched brows, she had noticed
Jan's slip.

'You're intimate with him?'

'Not really, I ... we ... well, formality does seem a
little out of place on a small ship,' Jan told her frankly.

Lydia smiled. 'Of course,' she agreed non-committaly. 'I'll admit I'm English enough to believe it's more important for a couple to be in love than to haggle over settlements. This cousin of yours, you say she's beautiful?'

'Oh very, she has most striking colouring.'

'But like most beautiful women, she's spoilt and selfish?'

'Not at all, though being much admired she has been a little indulged.' Jan was trying to be fair.

'Family loyalty,' Lydia suggested. 'She seems to be a bit capricious to act as she did. Does she love my son?'

Jan hesitated; the state of Renata's feelings towards Alex were not easy to define. 'He fascinates her,' she said at length, adding with more vigour : 'Of course she must love him, and if he wants her, he's got her. The little setback will have made them both keener.'

'Perhaps, but she doesn't sound to me the right wife for Alex. Men are such fools when it comes to choosing a mate.' Mrs Leandris' tone became dry. 'They go for looks and don't study character. The looks fade and they're stuck with the character.' She looked at Jan shrewdly. 'A nice steady girl like you appear to be would suit him much better.'

Jan blushed and lowered her eyes, but she retorted quickly :

'Girls like me, plain girls, have no appeal for men like Mr Leandris.'

'More's the pity.' She had guessed Jan's secret. 'Are you telling me you were alone for three days with Alex and he didn't make a pass at you?' she queried.

Jan's blush deepened and she became absorbed in the dregs in her coffee cup.

'Well, didn't he?' Lydia Leandris persisted.

'You evidently know your son very well,' Jan returned. 'If you must have it ... he did, but I know he
didn't mean anything, he was just bored with nothing
to do. Of course I didn't reciprocate.' Not entirely, she
assured herself, she *had* put up some resistance and
had escaped the logical conclusion.

'No?' Lydia looked unbelieving. 'You must be very
strong-minded.'

'Well, I'm not permissive,' Jan retorted with energy,
'and—well, look at me! For a man who has his pick
of lovelies, I wasn't likely to be a very great temptation.'

Lydia did, seeing and liking much about her visitor
that would have surprised Jan. The girl was loyal,
candid and seemingly truthful. Properly dressed and
groomed she might even be beautiful. She had good
bones and attractive colouring, but she would never
appear superficially pretty, she was not that type.

'Alex is astute enough to look below the surface,'
she said kindly. 'Beauty we know is only skin deep.
You're quite charming, my child.'

Jan winced. Must she always be taken to be younger
than her years?

'I wasn't charming to him,' she admitted. 'I called
him some awful names. I ... I don't like masterful
men.'

She still was not sure she liked Alex, but she loved
him, which was something quite different. Lydia's
critical regard was disconcerting her. Alex's mother was
no fool and would naturally assume she had fallen for
her son. But she had no intention of confiding in her,
let her surmise what she pleased, but once she had met

Renata she would understand Jan could not hold a candle to her.

At her mention of masterful men, Lydia laughed gaily, and her eyes went to a framed photograph standing on a side table of a handsome man with a look of Alex.

'You're a lot cleverer than you realise,' she said. 'Men can be surfeited with sugar. As for masterful men,' she indicated the photograph, 'my husband was a bit of a tyrant. A mingling of Greek and Turk so despotism was born in him, but I soon learned to manage him. It can be done, if you love.' Her blue eyes became very soft. 'I've never ceased to mourn for him.'

'You've got your son,' Jan said consolingly.

'Until another woman annexes him, and I'm hoping for a daughter-in-law who won't shut me out. I'm sure you never would, but this Renata ...' Lydia Leandris shook her head.

'You can't judge her until you've met her,' Jan pointed out, wondering if she had inadvertently painted an unflattering picture of her cousin. Renata was too easygoing to be jealous of a mother-in-law, but she would not give her a great deal of consideration. 'And I haven't got a drachma of dowry,' she went on, anxious to emphasise her ineligibility. 'I'm an orphan, dependent upon my uncle, except for the pittance he gives me for doing his typing. But I'm intending to launch out on my own, get an independent job as soon as I return to England and become a career girl.'

She could hardly expect Mrs Leandris to be interested in her plans, but she was anxious to make clear that she was not yearning after Alex.

'*When* you get back to England,' Lydia observed

significantly. 'For the moment you're my secretary and I must pay you a salary.'

'Of course not,' Jan cried. 'It's only a temporary arrangement, so that my uncle won't know that Alex ... er ...' she paused.

'Abducted you,' Lydia concluded for her.

'In mistake for Rena.'

'Which your uncle would deplore.'

'Could you expect him to do otherwise?'

'No, except that if he wants to secure Alex, he could have used the circumstances to put pressure on him to marry her,' Lydia remarked shrewdly. 'But I'm glad the plan misfired. Enforced marriages are not conducive to happiness, and I want Alex to be happy.'

'So do I,' Jan said sincerely.

She bore Alex no ill will for his treatment of her, and it was sheer bad luck that she had come to love him. He did not want her love and she had no wish to bestow it, but the thing had happened, and she was grateful to him for enriching her life. Whatever happened to her in the future, she would always have her brief association with him to look back upon, a glamorous memory to lighten the bleakness ahead.

As for Lydia's suggestion that she might make him a better wife than Renata, the idea was ludicrous; she was quite unfitted for such a position and he would never consider her seriously. To him she was plain Janet, an odd little creature whom it amused him to tease, and he had never wholly forgotten her first and freely expressed opinion of him. It had been a triumph for him to overcome her resistance to the point where she had responded to his lovemaking, and that was why he had done it, but she did not for one moment credit

that she was more to him than a diversion to while away
an idle hour. Lydia's attitude was prompted by her
wish for a malleable daughter-in-law, a mouselike
woman who would not question her supremacy in her
son's life, but she misjudged her guest, for Jan was
neither mouselike nor meek, though she might appear
insignificant. It was unfortunate that Mrs Leandris
seemed prejudiced against Renata without even having met her, but she might change her mind when she
saw her. She could not fail to realise that Renata Reynolds was ideally suited to preside over Alex's estab-
lishment and that she would impress his friends.

'You must help me to ensure it,' Lydia declared,
watching Jan closely.

The girl made a gesture of dissent. She did not
want to be further involved in the Alex-Renata compli-
cation. If she could have followed her own inclination,
she would have left for England there and then without seeing either of them again, but she could not do
so without assistance in her travel arrangements, the
necessary funds and her passport. At that moment she
was penniless and without credentials.

'You won't need any help from me,' she said. 'It's all
more or less settled.'

Renata would not hesitate now. Though she had
baulked at becoming Alex's mistress, she would jump
at being his wife. It was what she had angled for all
along, while Alex had committed himself too far to
draw back, unless he were the cad which Jan had
once thought, but no longer believed him to be.

'I've no further part to play,' she went on, striving
to speak lightly. 'I shall quietly fade out.'

Involuntarily a disconsolate note crept into her voice,

and her hostess noticed it. She eyed the girl with a
little inscrutable smile hovering about her still pretty
mouth at some secret thought of her own, but dropped
the subject and started to talk of other things.

They moved out on to the terrace where subse-
quently lunch was brought out to them on a trolley—
iced melon, shellfish salads and fruit. Jan tried not to
think of the meeting taking place at the airport, and to
concentrate on her novel surroundings. She was privileged to visit one of the most historic spots in Europe,
the gateway to the Mediterranean which had been a
focal point throughout the history of what had once
been known as Constantinople, and Lydia began to describe the glories of the Ottoman Empire which was
now shrunken and impoverished.

'You must be sure to visit the Topkapi Palace while
you're here,' she told her. 'It is now a museum, and
the collection of treasures there gives some idea of the
Sultan's former magnificence.'

Jan said she had done so, though at that moment she
was entirely indifferent to treasures past or present.

Lydia, it transpired, had acquired the Mediterranean
habit of taking a siesta during the hottest part of the
afternoon and advised her guest to do likewise. She
conducted her up to the room which had been prepared
for her. It was above the sitting room with a broad balcony outside its french windows overlooking the terrace. The balcony ran along the front of the upper floor
of the house, the rooms on either side of hers also
opening on to it, though it was divided from them
by low trellised fences. The room itself was furnished
elegantly with white and gilt French furniture, the
low wide bed covered with a lace coverlet, and there

was a bathroom connected to it.

'I hope you'll be comfortable in here,' Lydia said.

'It's lovely, much too good for a mere secretary.'

Lydia laughed. 'Don't be so humble. It pays to take all you're offered without qualifications, as if it were your right.'

'But I've no right to expect anything from you, and I'm grateful for your kindness,' Jan told her, suspecting a deeper meaning behind Lydia's words. Mrs Leandris could not know that the circumstances of Jan's life had taught her to expect little consideration from anybody. Her aunt, though vaguely kind, had impressed upon her that she owed her uncle's family service for giving her a home.

She noticed her case had been brought up, and when she was alone she opened it, hoping that her own luggage would soon arrive from the airport, since she had none of the necessities for her stay.

Renata's cloak was on top and she shook it out with a wry smile, recalling the occasion upon which she had borrowed it. How little she had foreseen what was going to happen! Underneath it was the shift dress in which she had come aboard, and the toilet things that she had used on the ship, also the nightdress Alex had made her don when he had threatened to strip her. Finally she came upon the chiffon and diamanté evening dress she had worn at Lesbos.

Ariadne must have been instructed to include the night gear, etc., in the case in the event of her own possessions being delayed, an act of thoughtfulness which caused her eyes to mist, for Alex must have instigated it. Contradictory creature, he considered her comfort, even while baiting her. But there was no need

to include the dress. She lifted it out and found pinned
to it a piece of paper on which was inscribed in a bold
sprawling hand:

'Please accept this small memento of a delightful
evening. I could not bear to see anyone else wearing it
after you had graced it. A.'

Jan stared at the writing for a long time. She had
not seen his calligraphy before and it was typical of the
man. What a generous gesture, but she could not accept
it. Somehow she must find a way to return his gift to
him; she could not allow him to give her clothes. Then
she recollected that the dress she was wearing was also
his. As soon as her own things arrived, she would make
a parcel of the borrowed garments and ask one of the
servants to deliver it to him. She fingered the skirt of
the dress a little wistfully. She had never owned anything so stylish, and even her inexperienced eye could
see it was a model gown, but it was impossible she
could ever wear it again.

But about that she changed her mind, for when she
came downstairs after a refreshing sleep which she
needed after her bad night, Lydia told her, over a cup
of tea, for she adhered to that English habit, that Alex
had telephoned to say he was bringing the Reynolds to
dine with them that night.

Jan's reaction to that news was an impulse to develop
a headache and plead that she was not up to attending a
dinner party, but Lydia divined her thought from her
expression and said firmly:

'You must support me, my dear. They're your relations and I'm sure your learned uncle will be formidable, so please, no excuses, and indeed you look much
better for your rest.'

So Jan overcame her cowardly wish to absent herself, though Jeremy was not at all formidable, as she hastened to assure her hostess. She would have to be reunited with her family some time, it was only that she shrank from seeing Alex and Renata together, but that was something she would have to become accustomed to, and Renata owed her some thanks. She and her father might even be pleased to see her.

'They are bringing your luggage with them,' Lydia told her. 'But I suppose you've something to wear tonight?'

Jan nodded. 'I have.'

CHAPTER SEVEN

DINNER was to be at a late hour, and it was dark when Jan went up to dress for it. There was an electric fire in her room, provided in case the night turned chill, and she rinsed out her nylon underwear and put it to dry in front of it while she bathed. The bathroom was furnished with various jars of bath essences and salts; Jan revelled in the scent of sandalwood from the liquid she poured into the bath. Hadn't Lydia told her to make the most of what was offered to her?

She had no option but to wear Alex's gift, for she could not shame her hostess by appearing in a day shift or the slightly soiled dress she had been wearing. It hurt her pride to do so, for it had occurred to her that Alex had bestowed it as a sop for his cavalier treatment of her, and as such she resented it. But he would not notice her appearance tonight with Renata present. Since there would be five of them she must resign herself to her usual position of odd man out, but at least she would be becomingly clad.

Jan had not Ariadne's skill with her hair, and finally she gave up her efforts to do it in the classic style and parting it in two long swathes, drew one over each shoulder, tying it with the silver ribbons which had been included with the dress.

When she came down, Lydia was already in the sitting room, wearing black, which was almost a uniform for Greek widows; a severely cut satin dress relieved by a splendid diamond necklace, and there were diamonds on her wrists, fingers and in her ears, but they were not large enough to be ostentatious, though they did indicate the Leandrises' wealth. Renata would be envious of them and hope to acquire some herself.

Lydia complimented Jan upon her appearance.

'So sweet and natural, child.'

Which did not please Jan at all, who wanted to appear sophisticated and did not consider herself a child. It was her hair which spoilt the dignity of her gown, and she wished again she had had it cut short. She wondered how old Lydia thought she was, but before she could enlighten her, Alex arrived with his guests. He was looking very distinguished in a black dinner jacket, and as soon as he entered the room, his virile personality seemed to pervade it. Jeremy was attired in a slightly crumpled suit and appeared very much the absent-minded professor, but Renata was a gorgeous vision in a golden sheath, her beautiful hair backcombed into a flaming aureole about her vivid face. The introductions were performed, and Jan saw Lydia look a little startled as Renata was presented to her.

Her eyes went past her to her son, who gave her an ironic smile. Renata's manner was almost gushing as she praised the house and her kindness in inviting them. This was Alex's mother and it was necessary to win her a probation, until the knot was tied.

Jeremy wandered over to Jan who was standing in the background.

'You were a naughty girl to sneak off like that,' he told her. 'We couldn't think where you'd got to until Alex's message arrived. I hope you're making yourself useful.'

'Very useful,' Lydia told him with a sly smile, over-hearing him.

Renata turned to stare at her cousin.

'Where on earth did you get that preposterous gown?'

'Oh, haven't you seen it before?' Jan asked with apparent nonchalance. 'I thought it was rather nice.'

'You couldn't have got it in Kusadasi.' Renata had recognised the Parisian line.

'No. It . . . it was a present.'

'Who from? You?' She looked at Lydia.

'No, from me.' Alex came to Jan's side. 'Since Jan left in such a hurry she forgot to pack a case, I lent her a dress out of the communal wardrobe, and it suited her so well I told her to keept it.'

'I don't see why she needed an evening dress, and one like that is most unsuitable.' Renata's eyes narrowed. 'When did you arrive in Istanbul, Jan?'

'This morning,' Jan told her guilelessly.

'This morning? Where on earth have you been since leaving Kusadasi?'

'I had urgent business which necessitated a call at

Lesbos,' Alex again intervened. 'That delayed us.'

'In spite of your mother's urgent need of a secretary?' Renata sneered.

'The firm's business takes priority,' he returned.

Jan was dismayed by her cousin's obvious hostility. It was in her service that she had been carried off in the *Artemis* and she should be sympathetic, not angry. The green eyes were still eyeing her suspiciously, as Renata said:

'Then I hope you behaved discreetly and stayed down below while the yacht was in port.'

'I took her out to dine at Mithimna,' Alex informed her. 'The poor girl deserved some entertainment since she was ready to help my mother out in an emergency.'

His eyes met Renata's with a definite challenge. Both knew what a fabrication that emergency was, and Renata was furious. Jan realised with a feeling of shock that she was jealous, jealous of herself and Alex in a situation which she had brought about by her own cowardice.

'Let us go into dinner,' Lydia interposed, sensing a strained atmosphere. 'Alex, give me your arm.'

Having thus forestalled Renata's movement towards her son, Lydia marched on ahead leaving the other three to follow.

The dining room was at the back of the house, being mostly filled with a vast sideboard of marble-topped ormolu and the dining table. This was laid with silver, crystal and vases of flowers, and lit by a magnificent chandelier. Lydia sat at the head of her table with Alex at its foot, with Renata on his right and Jan on his left. Jeremy was placed between his daughter and his hostess. Renata threw a satisfied glance round at the appointments of the room. It was not to her taste, but it bore witness to the Leandrises' affluence. Jan's presence opposite to her seemed to offend her, and after glancing at her disparagingly she returned to the attack.

'What an absurd childish way to do your hair! Why not your usual bun, that at least is dignified.'

Jan flushed miserably and looked at her plate.

'I like it,' Alex said firmly, and that silenced Renata.

Jan gave him a grateful look and he smiled at her. Renata noticed the smile and frowned, but she left Jan alone for the rest of the meal, chattering brightly to Alex about her impressions of the country. He listened to her politely, with a little satirical smile, ignoring Jan's presence beside him. Since her uncle and Lydia were discussing Ephesian art, Jan ate her food in silence, which was her usual fate. She had never resented being overlooked before, but after she had been the sole focus of Alex's attention, his neglect was painful. She told herself it was what she must expect, and tried to keep her eyes from straying to his handsome profile. She had little appetite and refused most of the rich dishes offered to her by soft-footed servants, but naturally nobody noticed, and she was thankful for that.

Back in the sitting room, coffee was served to them, and then, suddenly putting down her cup, Renata addressed her cousin.

'You borrowed my cloak when you rushed off. I hope you haven't lost it.'

'Of course I haven't, it's upstairs.'

'Then let's go and get it,' Renata commanded. 'I'll find it useful in this place.'

Jan rose reluctantly, knowing this was an excuse to speak to her alone, and she dreaded what Renata was going to say. As she passed him, Alex looked up at her with a glint in his eyes, and she turned her head away.

'Want me to come and support you?' he said under his breath.

She shook her head dumbly and led the way out of the room.

In her bedroom, Renata turned on her.

'You rotten little cheat!' she blazed, her green eyes sparkling. 'Trying to steal a march on me! Sneaking off with Alex when you pretended you couldn't stand him. What lies did you tell him to persuade him to take you?'

Jan went very white. 'You've got it all wrong, Rena. I had to go on the yacht to deliver your message because Alex wasn't on the quay.'

'You could have given it to the sailors.'

'They didn't understand English.'

'Well then, when you got on board, you'd only to speak up and he'd have had you put ashore again.'

'He wasn't there. I was locked up in a cabin until the yacht sailed.'

Renata stared at her incredulously.

'Do you expect me to believe that yarn?'

'But it's the truth, Rena. He thought I was you and he ... he wanted to keep intruders out until he was ready to come to you.' Jan began to giggle. 'You should have seen Alex's expression when he opened the door and saw me standing there!'

Somewhat mollified, Renata's face cleared, and she too began to laugh. 'I bet it was a shock!' Her brows drew together. 'But he could have sent you back from Lesbos.'

'There didn't seem to be any transport, and as you were to meet him here, he said it wasn't worth while.'

'I suppose there was reason in that,' Renata agreed reluctantly. 'But to accept a dress ...' She glowered at the green chiffon.

'I'd nothing with me,' Jan reminded her. 'Only the frock I came aboard in.'

'You didn't need anything else if you were locked in your cabin.'

'I wasn't, not after the first night.'

'Oh yes, dinner at Mithima—most indiscreet.' Renata's eyes narrowed spitefully. 'Couldn't he find something better looking if he needed a companion? But don't tell me he bought that dress in Lesbos. It has Paris written all over it.'

Jan explained about the communal wardrobe and Renata laughed jeeringly.

'How gullible can you be! Of course all those clothes were bought for me. That dress is my thing and my colour. I'd look a darned sight better in it than you do.'

Jan felt she had indeed been gulled, and Alex's message was an insult. He had expected that she would wear the garment that evening, and Renata would guess for whom it had been intended. He wanted to show her what she had forfeited by standing him up. Of course the whole set-up, the beautiful cabin, the array of gowns, even the underwear had been prepared for Renata. Alex, with his subtle revenges, had derived satisfaction from her occupancy of it and her use of the clothes, knowing how it would sting Renata when

she was told about it, as Jan in her simplicity would
be sure to do. Her former antipathy against Alexandros
Leandris revived. The man was a callous brute. Every
action of his since leaving Kusadasi had been motivated
by a desire to spite Renata. By flattery he had ensured
that she would wear the dress, and his support downstairs had not been kindness but aimed at her cousin.
Renata had to be punished for rejecting him before he
reinstated her.

'Then you'd better take it,' Jan said calmly, disguising her indignation. 'There are several other oddments
in that case which I shan't need now you've brought
my things.' She smiled wryly. 'Since they were meant
for you, you must have them. Take the case as well.'

Renata glanced curiously at Jan, surprised that she
was so willing to relinquish her spoils.

'Green chiffon isn't your thing,' she remarked, and
went eagerly to inspect the contents of the case. She
pulled out the silk nightdress. 'No, this certainly is not
you, but are you sure you don't want them? You
haven't many pretty things.'

'As you say, they aren't me,' Jan returned stonily.
She did not want anything that reminded her of Alex.
She untied the sash at her waist. 'This dress doesn't
even fit me.' She let it fall about her feet and Renata
snatched it up.

'What a way to treat a model gown! Sure, it's
wasted on you.'

She held it against herself and the colour brought
out the green in her eyes. Jan felt a pang, she had
thought the dress became her, but it would look vastly
different upon Renata. But it had always been so. Anything pretty and decorative enhanced her cousin's

beauty and emphasised her own plainness. That was why, long ago, she had given up bothering about her looks. Once when she was about eight years old they had been given identical party dresses and Renata looked liked the fairy on top of a Christmas tree, but when Jan had caught sight of her own image, her plain little face and straight brown hair done in unbecoming plaits, rising from the lace yoke of the frock, had given her a shock. She looked like an ugly travesty of her cousin. The contrast was too painful for a sensitive child and she had refused to go to the party, saying she felt sick. Her aunt, with scant sympathy and no inkling of what had upset her, put her to bed before accompanying her own child. Renata, kinder then, had brought back the cracker and small present allocated to her with their hostess's regrets and commiserated with Jan for missing all the fun.

'It was very unfair that you should be taken ill.'

'Yes, it was very unfair that nature had made one child a beauty, and the other an ugly duckling, as she had described herself to Alex, but it was no one's fault and in time she had become resigned to it. To her credit she had never been jealous of Renata's loveliness and she was not so now, green chiffon was created for girls like her cousin, but she did resent Alex's duplicity. To declare that he could not bear to see anyone else wearing the dress which he had chosen for Renata, and must have been envisaging her in it all the time she was wearing it, was an unnecessary piece of insincerity.

In response to Renata's remark she returned:

'It is. I ... I don't care for fancy things. But you can't blame me for what happened. You know you begged me to take your message because you were scared stiff.'

'I only had a moment's panic,' Renata declared. 'You shouldn't have taken any notice of it. Every girl has nerves before getting married. It's a big step to take, especially to a foreigner, and if you'd had more savvy you'd have understood. There was no need for this ... this masquerade of yours, all I needed was a little re-assurance. Since Alex afterwards sent for me, it shows he's discovered he can't do without me.' She preened herself. 'We'll be married in London, and we'll live in Athens. Alex says he's got a lovely house there, more modern than this mausoleum.'

Jan, arrayed only in her slip, was repacking the bor-rowed suitcase, and included the blue and white day dress she had been wearing. Renata had convinced herself that Alex had meant marriage all along, which was not what she had said in Kusadasi. He must have been more definite when he met her again, and after the enforced hours spent in her own company, her cousin's glorious beauty must have struck him afresh and wrung a proposal from him. It was as she had anticipated, but her heart felt like lead. She had never accepted before that Renata was spoilt and selfish, her love for her cousin had blinded her to her faults, but Renata's un-just accusations, her wilful misunderstanding of the difficult situation Jan had been in for her sake, which deserved gratitude, not blame, was revealing a new and unpleasant side of her character. Not only was she jealous, she was being malicious.

'It's unfortunate you have to stay in the same house as he is,' Renata went on, for she could not rid herself of the suspicion that Jan was trying to annex Alex, though she could have no hope of success. 'It must be very embarrassing for him when he must be longing to be rid of you, but as we can't tell Daddy the truth, I suppose we'll have to continue with the silly secretary story for the time being.' Her gaze sharpened. 'Does Mrs Leandris know the truth?'

'Naturally,' Jan's tone was dry, 'since she doesn't need a secretary.'

Regretfully she placed the controversial green dress last in the case and closed the lid.

'I wonder how Alex bamboozled her into accepting you,' Renata exclaimed. 'She looks a sensible woman, but he can be a cunning devil when he wants his way. It's not right you should impose on her. Perhaps it would be better to confess everything to Daddy.'

'Do, if you think he'll appreciate your conduct,' Jan told her bluntly. 'But I shan't disguise the fact that you were going to elope with Alex without a promise of marriage, if only to protect myself.'

Some of Renata's confidence faded. 'He wouldn't believe you,' she said doubtfully. 'He was always sure Alex meant to marry me.'

'Yes, but *you* weren't,' Jan said brutally.

'Come off it, Rena, you were in a blue funk that evening because Alex was *not* going to marry you and you'd just realised the full implications of what you were about to do.'

All the colour drained from Renata's face and she slapped Jan's cheek.

'How dare you say that!'

'I dare because it's the truth and you know it.'

Jan turned away, gently touching her face where Renata had struck her. Her slap had been hard, but it did not hurt her nearly as much as her injustice.

Presently, in a shaky voice, Renata asked:

'Did he, when you were afloat together, tell you he wouldn't marry me?'

'No.' Jan wished she could say yes, Renata deserved that, but she could not be anything but honest. 'He said some foul things about women in general as he often does, which would indicate that he's been mixed up with some bitchy types in his time, but he implied that he was contemplating marrying you. You see, he needs a wife to produce heirs, so why not you?'

She had the satisfaction of seeing her cousin wince at her plain speaking. Renata did not care for children.

'If he's thinking I'm a sort of brood mare, he's got another think coming,' she declared heatedly.

'It'll be expected of you, Rena.' Jan was human enough to enjoy Renata's dismay.

'Oh well, I suppose I *could* go through with it *once*,' Renata conceded. She stroked her body lovingly. 'To be swollen and disfigured ... ugh!'

'Most women consider it's worth it,' Jan remarked.

'A lot of women haven't any figure to lose,' Renata retorted. 'Of course, being plain you wouldn't understand my feelings.'

'No, I don't.' Jan herself would love to have a child, especially if Alex were its father. 'But cheer up, you may discover you possess latent maternal instincts.'

'As likely as flying to Mars,' Renata returned scornfully. 'But I'm sure Alex will give me some wonderful jewels if I present him with a son.' She gave Jan an arch look. 'Would you say he loves me?'

Jan laughed brittlely. 'Mr Leandris' feelings are a closed book, I don't think he's got any tender ones. He admires you, he wants to possess you, and if that's enough for you, you'll get him.'

All unbidden, the recollection of Stephanos and the gentleness in Alex's voice when he spoke to him recurred to her. The man was capable of softer feelings, but she did not think Renata could arouse them. She would make him a satisfactory wife, she reflected a little bitterly, he would be proud of her looks, subdue her will and get himself heirs on her body, while Renata would have her fill of luxury and expensive baubles, but as for love, that elusive precious thing, there would be little of that in their union.

Renata had recovered her self-assured poise, which Jan had temporarily shattered.

'Of course I've got him,' she declared triumphantly. 'I'm sorry I slapped you, but you are irritating at times. You always blurt out facts without any finesse, which I believe you call being honest, but I consider lack of tact. I don't think there's much love around, it's something I've never experienced.'

She moved restlessly across to the window and fingered the louvred blind. 'Poor Denis,' she murmured, more to herself than to Jan. 'He was sweet, but he couldn't give me what I want. Alex will.' She swung round to face her cousin. 'Alex and I'll rub along as well as most couples and I'll get used to him in time. Are you going to come down again?'

Jan shook her head. 'I haven't unpacked and I've nothing to put on. Please tell Mrs Leandris I'm tired and I've got a bit of a headache, so I've gone to bed. I don't suppose Uncle Jeremy and Alex will notice I'm not there.'

'Quite likely,' Renata agreed. 'Daddy's so vague, and

Alex has no thought for anyone but me.' She threw Jan a challenging look as if daring her to deny it. 'Put the case outside your door and I'll get someone to fetch it. Goodnight, Jan.'

When she had gone, Jan began to unpack her luggage which had been brought up while she was at dinner. She was tired and her head did ache. She felt a great longing for her own country where it was cool and green. Istanbul and the Bosphorus were beautiful, but it seemed to her excited fancy that there was something sensual and decadent about the atmosphere, an aura of past sins and excesses which was an incitement to passion of which she desired no further experience. Renata's attitude had wounded her deeply. They had always been like sisters; her simplicity had not yet learned that the commonest cause for a rift between women, however close, was a joint interest in the same man, but she would have denied strenuously that she had any interest in Alexandros Leandris, though it would not have been quite true, and at that moment she was hating him for disrupting her life. She thought regretfully of the state of placid calm in which she had existed before she had met him, but which she feared she would never be able to regain. The Janet Reynolds who had disembarked at Istanbul was not the same girl who had boarded the *Artemis* at Kusadasi. If it meant she was growing up, it was a painful process.

She hung her plain dresses in the wardrobe provided; she did possess a semi-evening dress, a dark red affair which did not suit her, and she could imagine Alex's look of distaste if he saw her in it. It would be a sad comedown after the green chiffon. But his interest in her appearance had only been perfunctory, though she could improve it now she had regained her cheques, but it was not worth while buying any more summer clothes with her return to England imminent, and autumn ahead. She owned one becoming garment, a caftan-style dressing gown which she had bought in Kusadasi on an extravagant impulse, in a rich shade of blue with gold braid. She slipped it on and put the alien case outside her door as Renata had requested.

Due to her siesta, she was not at all sleepy and the room felt close. She opened the windows wide and went out on to the balcony seeking a breath of air. It was a substantial structure built of cedarwood, enclosed by intricate latticework which formed a balustrade. It was high enough for her to rest her elbows upon it as she gazed out at the waterway. The moon was rising behind the Anatolian mountains, throwing a luminous radiance into the sky. It occurred to her that the latticework had once covered the whole balcony, for it was an old house, and the view through its meshes was all its female inmates were allowed to see of the outside world. Such incarceration was revolting to a Western mind, but doubtless Alex would have approved of it. Alex! She must not allow her mind to keep turning towards him. She stayed there a long time, while the house sank into silence as its mistress and the servants retired, after the departure of the visitors. Gradually her taut nerves relaxed, as she surveyed the dark water and the moon, and with a little sigh she turned away to re-enter her room.

'Jan!'

She stopped as if turned to stone, her heart racing. Vaguely she had supposed that Alex would escort the Reynolds back to the Hilton, overlooking the fact that he was staying in his mother's house. His unmistakable utterance of her name had the eerie effect of a cry from limbo. Then she saw a dark shape standing on the balcony next to hers, divided from her by a low partition. The room behind him was not illuminated and he was only a shadow in which the red eye of the cheroot he was smoking glowed ominously. With almost a sense of shock she realised he must be occupying the bedroom next to hers.

He threw the stub of his cheroot over the balcony parapet and it described a wide arc, dropping sparks as it fell. His action penetrated her numbed senses and she cried reprovingly:

'You shouldn't do that! There might be someone below.'

'Probably is, waiting hopefully to retrieve it,' he returned. 'Why did you run away without saying goodnight?'

'I didn't think my absence would be noticed.'

'That's no excuse for lack of manners. Naturally I noticed—I'm not unobservant.'

'I didn't mean to be rude,' she said coldly. 'I sent a message by Rena. Since I was up here there didn't seem much point in coming down again.'

'Ah yes, the devoted cousins came up for a heart-to-heart.' There was a mocking note in his voice. 'Renata must have been eager to express her thanks for all you had endured on her behalf.'

'Of course.' She had no intention of revealing to him what Renata had said. 'I thought you'd gone back with her. I'd no idea you were next door.'

'There was no need to escort them, Reynolds had

hired a car, and this is my home, when I'm here.'

'Yes, I'd forgotten. It's late, so I'll wish you a belated goodnight.'

Jan moved towards the open door of her room in which she had left the light burning, but he agilely climbed over the low barrier and stood barring her way. She saw then that he had undressed and was attired in a dark silk robe which made him look very tall. Since his face was in shadow she could not see his expression, but he looked intimidating.

'That's quite a becoming garment you've got on,' he remarked, for the light spilling through the doorway illuminated her figure though he was a silhouette. 'Apparently you have some dress sense, though it doesn't extend to the rest of your wardrobe. Why don't you let your cousin choose your clothes? She'd know what would become you.'

'Rena is not interested in my appearance, and apparently you choose hers. She was sure the dress you lent me was selected for her.'

'What the hell are you talking about?' he demanded.

'You know perfectly well. When next you see it, it'll be on the person for whom it was intended.'

'So Renata has been acquisitive . . .'

She interrupted him quickly, not wanting to prolong the painful subject:

'Would you mind going back to your room, Mr Leandris? It's late and I want to go to bed.'

'Alone?'

'That sort of remark is automatic with you, isn't it? But I'm very tired, I've had a trying day and I've no energy to fence with you tonight.'

'My dear girl, I've no wish to fight you. You shall go to your virginal bed, but first won't you say goodnight properly?'

'I have said goodnight, and in the only way that's proper between you and me.'

'We may have different ideas about that,' he countered.

'Oh, go away!' she exclaimed irritably. Turning round, she walked back to the balustrade and stood with her back to him staring blindly out to sea. Why must he persist in baiting her? He had got his Renata, who surely was enough for any man. She leaned her elbows on top of the parapet and covered her face with her hands.

'Jan.' He was beside her, though she had not heard him move. Gently he took her hands away from her face. 'Not crying, are you? I'd hate to make you weep.'

The tenderness in his voice almost had that effect, but she stiffened. It was all put on; if he could not get round her one way he would try another. He was Alexandros the Conqueror, and even plain Janet could not be allowed to escape. She looked up at him defiantly:

'No, I'm not crying, but we're not on your yacht now, we're in your mother's house, and I'm sure she'd be shocked if she knew where you were.'

'She wouldn't, she has a modern outlook.'

'Well, I haven't, if by that you mean she'd condone permissiveness. What do you want with me, Alex? You know our ... our association is ended.'

He was staring down into her upturned face and in the half light his eyes seemed luminous. They really

were cats' eyes, she thought irrelevantly. But she
must not yield to his charisma.

'I'm sorry to hear you say that,' he told her. 'As for
what I want ... you know that, but you won't give it
to me.'

'Certainly not, when you're going to marry someone else!'

'Would *you* marry me if I asked you?'

She snatched her hands free. 'Again certainly not.'

'Might I ask why? I don't think I'm repulsive to
you.'

'Oh, Alex, do leave me alone!' she cried wildly,
nearly at the end of her endurance. He was so near, his
shoulder touching hers, and his familiar magnetism
was having its usual effect upon her, but honour,
Renata, her self-respect were barriers not to be overcome for a moment's gratification, and as for Alex,
he was behaving reprehensibly, but that was nothing
new.

'I may be homely and dowdy, but ... Oh, do go
away!'

He slipped an arm about her shoulders.

'Poor little Jan, you really are exhausted,' he said
kindly. 'Kiss me goodnight and I'll let you go.'

'No, Alex, your kisses belong elsewhere.'

'But you're going to be my little cousin. Don't
cousins kiss?'

The words smote her, she could not look upon him
as a kinsman, but to continue to deny him would only
provoke a demonstration she did not want. She knew
his persistence.

'Oh, very well,' she said ungraciously, and held up
her face.

He drew her closer and gently touched her lips. The contact produced no sudden flare of passion as it had done upon former occasions. She was too weary and he ... he belonged to Renata now. With a shamed regret for the death of his passion, she had to accept that he meant what he had said. She was to be his little cousin now, a creature to be treated with condescending affection, and she could not bear it.

With his arm still about her shoulders he guided her back towards her room, and on its threshold he removed it.

'Sleep well ... Jan.'

He gently pushed her inside and closed the doors behind her. The action was symbolical, the finish of whatever if anything had been between them.

Blindly Jan groped her way towards her bed and flung herself down upon it. She did not know how she was going to endure the next few days, seeing Alex every morning, knowing only a wall divided them at night. She clenched her hands in an agony of loss, until her common sense reasserted itself. How could she lose what she had never had? Nor should she grieve for a man who had in all his dealings with her shown himself to be tyrannical and unfeeling. Between Renata and his business their future contacts would be few, and Jeremy could not stay long in Istanbul.

The habit of years reasserted itself. She was plain Janet Reynolds whom no one considered and everyone made use of. Tomorrow she would revert to her dowdy dresses and her hair in a bun, and if she found Alex was at home, she would feign illness or stay in her room. When she reached England she would strike out on her own and create a new image of herself, and with that consoling thought to sustain her, she fell asleep.

Outside the moon shone brightly on the Bosphorus and the dark head of the man who leant over his balcony smoking innumerable cheroots, throwing the stubs on to the terrace to be collected by enterprising native boys before anyone was astir in the morning. Jan was not the only one who had problems to solve.

CHAPTER EIGHT

No pretence of illness was necessary, for Jan found that Alex left the house early before she had finished the coffee brought to her room and did not return until she had gone to bed. Business occupied his day, Lydia told her, and the evenings presumably were devoted to taking Renata out. There was plenty of night life in Istanbul which would appeal to Renata after her quiet sojourn in Kusadasi. Time hung heavy on Jan's hands, for she was used to being busy for most of the day. Lydia was immersed in her own concerns and beyond typing a few notes for her, there was little Jan could do to help her. As it was the permanent secretary, Maria, eyed her malevolently, suspecting she might be superseded, and was deaf to Jan's assurances that her presence was only temporary. What was so trying was that his enforced leisure provided no distraction from her thoughts of Alex and her yearning to see him again. They were living in the same house, but he avoided her as assiduously as she kept out of his way. It would be sheer folly to seek to encounter him, for, absorbed in Renata, he had probably forgotten Jan's existence and would have nothing to say to her. Her uncle was equally neglectful, as he never came to the house by the Bosphorus. If he needed any clerical work doing, Alex must have provided him with a typist. During the three days that elapsed since her arrival, Jan had plenty of time to reflect upon her redundancy and she was impatient to return to London and set about finding a congenial job.

She had dinner with Mrs Leandris in the evenings, and was on edge all the time in case Alex appeared, but he never did. Lydia's conversation was impersonal for the most part, though she did try to draw Jan out about her former life, but there was little to tell her, it had been so uneventful. Lunch Jan ate in solitary grandeur, as her hostess was usually out. She had little energy for sightseeing, for the weather was hot and it was dull doing it on her own.

Coming down on the fourth morning, arrayed in the most presentable of her cotton frocks, for she had lost all inclination to purchase something more dressy, she was surprised and disconcerted to find Alex sprawling in a lounger on the terrace. He sprang up as she halted in the doorway of the french window, uncertain whether to advance or retreat. Her heart had leaped at the sight of him, and as she half turned, he came towards her evidently intending to intercept her. He was wearing shorts and a sleeveless shirt, and the informal garb revealed his long, supple limbs which for so dark a man showed very little hair and were as smooth as the marble of which the statues of his ancestors were made. Jan disliked hirsute men, and Alex could have modelled for Apollo or Narcissus. She became aware of her shapeless lemon shift and knotted hair, and was sure she was appearing at her worst, and his expression bore that out.

'So you've reverted to the prim spinster of Kusadasi days,' he observed, and he made spinster sound like a dirty word.

'I ... I thought you'd have gone to work,' Jan stammered inadequately, every nerve in her body conscious of his presence. 'Is it a holiday ... or something?'

'Not that I know of. Missed me?' The yellow cat's eyes were probing.

She had missed him unbearably, but that she could not confess.

'Not really, there's been too much to do and see,' she said evasively, though it was not true, and his face went blank. His hands went to her head, loosening her hair so that it fell about her shoulders, and he stepped back to view the result.

'That's a little better, though it makes you look about twelve. Are you sure you're not mistaken about your age?'

'Quite sure.' She gathered up her stray locks in one hand. 'I've decided I'm going to have all this cut off.'

'Don't you dare! I like it.'

'It's inconvenient, and soon you'll be far away, so it won't affect you.' Inadvertently a note of desolation crept into her voice, and Alex marked it with a gleam of satisfaction in his eyes.

'Don't you be too sure of that.'

Ignoring this remark, Jan walked sedately to a distant canvas chair, and seating herself, tried unsuc-

cessfully to knot up her hair again, but her pins and
grips were scattered, and letting it fall again, she folded
her hands demurely in her lap and said severely:

'For an engaged man you're showing too much interest in my appearance, Mr Leandris.'

'Is an engaged man necessarily blind?'

'Yes, to all but his fiancée's charms.'

Alex laughed merrily. 'Jan, Jan, where do you get
your ideas from?' He indicated the lounger. 'Come and
sit over here instead of isolating yourself. We can't talk
with the width of the terrace between us.'

Jan declined this invitation with a shake of her head.

'Are you officially engaged yet?' she demanded
anxiously.

'I'm never officially anything.'

She sighed; he was being evasive.

'You're prevaricating,' she accused him. 'I like
situations to be defined in black and white.'

'In my case, they're always black, aren't they?
Come over here.'

He seated himself on the lounger, which was of the
hammock variety with a double seat and a canopy to
shade it from the sun. It swung gently as his weight
came down upon it. He patted the space beside him
invitingly.

'I'm quite comfortable where I am.'

'That you're not. The sun is scorching you. Must I
come and fetch you?'

There was a faint menace in his tone and Jan glanced
apprehensively towards the house wondering if Mrs
Leandris was watching them. Alex caught the direction
of her glance and grinned.

'My mother's out,' he informed her. 'The servants

are about their business, or should be, so there's no one to see you if you imagine you're being indiscreet. Come along.'

Jan rose reluctantly. She knew him well enough to be sure he would carry out his threat if she continued to be obdurate. It was more dignified to comply than be dragged across the terrace! She sat down as far away from him as the double seat allowed.

'What a tyrant you are!' she sighed.

He grinned. 'Chauvinist pig?' he suggested.

'Exactly.'

He leaned back in his corner regarding her sensuously.

'You look pale, little one, the heat tries you?'

'A little, and I'm finding my position a bit difficult. I'll be thankful to get back to England. How long does Uncle intend to stay here?'

Alex shrugged his shoulders. 'You'd better ask him.'

'I never see him.'

Alex picked up a strand of her hair and became absorbed in winding it round his finger.

'He neglects you?'

'I suppose he's got other things to think about, you know he forgets all practical matters when he's interested in something.'

'And I, of course, have only time for Renata.'

'That's as it should be.'

'Well, eventually we may get round to considering your predicament. It's no great hardship, Jan, to spend a few days relaxing in this beautiful place.'

'But I feel it's time I was doing something,' she protested.

'Such as?'

'Looking for a job.'

'A job?' He raised his brows. 'You don't need a job, you live with your uncle, don't you?'

'There's no future for me with Uncle Jeremy. It's time I struck out on my own.'

'I don't wish you to go out to work,' he told her, frowning. 'I've other plans for you.'

'But I'm no responsibility of yours,' she returned. 'Even if you are going to be my cousin. I'm quite capable of fending for myself, thank you very much.' She moved her head. 'Please let go of my hair, you're hurting me.'

He gave her hair a quick tug. 'As you deserve to be.'

'What have I done now?' She pinched his fingers to make him free her.

'Been singularly obtuse,' he told her, releasing her hair.

Jan swept her locks together and threw them back over her shoulder out of his reach. She was very conscious of his thigh, only inches from her own, and the shapely brown arm now lying across her lap. Her heart was beating fast, and she could not raise her eyes to meet his mocking gaze.

'You, as usual, are behaving abominably,' she said sharply.

'But entirely in character?' he suggested.

'Where's Rena?' Jan asked to divert him.

Again he shrugged. 'Shopping, I believe.'

That also was entirely in character.

'I knew she couldn't resist the bazaar,' Jan observed. 'But why aren't you with her? She shouldn't be wandering about alone.'

'She isn't alone, she's found kindred spirits in the hotel, and I loathe shopping.'

'The presence of the beloved should sweeten it.'

'Not when the beloved is so engrossed in her purchases that she has no time for me except to demand the amount in my wallet.'

'Rena is extravagant,' Jan admitted, not liking his tone. 'But doesn't it give you pleasure to indulge her?'

'I'm ready to indulge anyone when I'm sure of recompense.'

'Don't pretend to be mercenary! Rena will repay you in many ways!'

'Will she?'

'But of course.'

There was something here which puzzled her. It was not like Alex to play the laggard lover, nor to grudge expenditure. She looked down at the bare arm lying across her lap, the hand belonging to it, lightly pressing her thigh. Little tremors ran through her nerves. Firmly she removed it, and he let it fall by his side between them, while the cat's eyes searched her face questioningly.

'There are some women even I find difficult to fathom,' he complained. 'And I do not welcome a rebuff.'

'The all-conquering male?' she jeered. Surely he understood Renata by now. 'Rena would never rebuff you.'

He gave an impatient sigh. 'You're being stupid, Jan ... what else did she do when she refused to join me on the *Artemis*?'

'Is that still rankling? I thought it was all forgiven and forgotten, now you're engaged.'

'We aren't engaged.'

'Then in God's name what are you waiting for?' Jan cried in consternation. 'Why else did you arrange for her to come here?'

Alex gave her a reproving look.

'There's no hurry,' he drawled. 'Choosing one's life partner is not a matter for haste. Surely you, my cautious Jan, appreciate that.'

She did not, she was bewildered and dismayed. Why was Alex stalling at this late date?

'You're committed . . .' she began.

'Am I?'

'Oh, Alex, don't be so perverse!' she exclaimed impatiently. 'You know Uncle Jeremy and your mother are expecting the announcement hourly. You've given us all to understand you mean to marry her.'

'You don't mind?' He looked at her intently.

'I'll mind very much if you let her down. You . . . you've compromised her!'

Alex smiled sardonically.

'I don't think it's possible to compromise the modern miss,' he said cynically. 'Come to that, you might complain, in fact you did hint that I'd compromised you, but you don't seem to expect me to marry you.'

'That's entirely different,' Jan returned. 'I'm not worried about my reputation. Even if anyone in England gets to know about our . . . little adventure, what one does on holiday doesn't count.'

Alex laughed. 'So your high principles allow you that much latitude? But if there's any doubt about a slur on your fair name, I'm quite willing to put on a quixotic act to save it from being smirched.'

Mocking, teasing and yet with a subtle undercurrent,

but had she succeeded in convincing him of her indifference? If he suspected it was an act, then he was
being cruel to taunt her by making such tantalising
but unrealistic suggestions. Alex was cruel where
women were concerned, as if he had a grudge against
her sex, when in fact it had been more than kind to
him.

'You know perfectly well that a union between you
and me would be utterly disastrous,' she said coldly.
'We're quite unsuited, and I assure you it's not in the
least necessary to put such a strain upon your chivalry.'

'Up to now you've refused to believe I possessed
any.'

'Oh, I've revised my first impressions of you quite
considerably,' she admitted.

'That's something.'

He leaned back, regarding her between slitted lids.
The heat was increasing as the sun approached the
meridian, the terrace was bathed in golden light and
the scarlet geraniums in the stone urns were turned
to liquid fire. The Bosphorus was flecked with sequins
as the sunlight danced upon it. The place drowsed in
sensuous languor, and Jan smoothed down the limp
folds of her dress with a feeling of unease. She could
not conceive why Alex was lingering with her when
Renata must be expecting him, nor find any reason for
his evocative remarks. She remembered he had once
said vinegar was stimulating after a diet of sweets, or
words to that effect, and he seemed to enjoy pitting his
wits against hers, but they had had plenty of verbal
battles before, so that was no novelty. He had claimed
her as a cousin, but men did not dally with cousins
when more attractive metal awaited them. She wished

fervently that Lydia would return and divert him. She was reminded of the fable of the boys who stoned the frogs. The frogs complained that what was amusement to the boys was death to them. Alex found diversion in baiting her, but with every moment in his company increasing her yearning towards him, she felt her control might snap if it went on much longer.

'But your reassessment hasn't reached the point of considering I'm ... lovable?' Alex asked, and the hooded glance became eager.

Jan veiled her own eyes with her lashes, unable to sustain that piercing regard. He did seem to want a truthful answer. Long ago, she and Renata had decided that Alex might inspire a passionate devotion, but lovable seemed too cosy a word to apply to him, and why should he ask such a question of her who had every reason to despise him ... except that she did not? Then it flashed into her mind what had prompted it.

'I'm sure Rena has got over her fear and has come to love you,' she said reassuringly.

He made a grimace.

'Can't you answer a straight question without dragging in your cousin?' he demanded.

'But it's Rena's love you want,' she pointed out. 'And you, Alex, have you come to love her? Oh, I know you want her, but that's not quite the same thing. It would make such a difference to your happiness if you have,' she finished hurriedly, seeing his brows draw together and fearing she had been impertinent.

'You're being maudlin,' he returned. 'I'm rather past romantic love. Oh, I was in and out of love often enough when I was a youth, boys always are, but now

I'm mature I've done with such folly.'

He threw her an almost inimical look.

'But it's nothing to be ashamed of,' Jan protested. She gave him a shrewd glance. 'Does your masculine arrogance feel that to fall in love is a weakness so you won't confess it?'

He sprang to his feet with a swift agile movement and striding to the nearest urn, began to strip the petals from the blooms with a fierce ruthlessness.

'Don't!' Jan cried, horrified by such wanton destruction. 'Those poor flowers haven't done you any harm.'

He swung round to face her and the red petals surrounding him looked like drops of blood.

'Like many an innocent I've ravished,' he gritted savagely.

'Rubbish, why do you want to make out you're a villain?'

'Still trying to whitewash me?' he sneered. He broke off a spray of bloom and twirled it between his fingers. 'You're still so young, Jan, while I ...' He stopped and looked away across the water.

'Rena is no older,' she pointed out.

'In years perhaps, but she was born sophisticated.' He threw away the spray of flowers. 'Ridiculous as it seems, I find I'm still capable of falling in love.'

'Of course you are. I believe no one is immune at any age, and adult love is stronger and more stable than youthful infatuations.' She spoke with a quaint air of wisdom that caused Alex to smile. Looking at him questioningly, she went on: 'Do you mean that you've really fallen in love with Rena? That would be ... splendid.'

Her voice faltered. If he had it would do much to ensure Renata's future happiness, but her own heart was protesting that while she had faced a marriage of convenience with equanimity, Alex's rhapsodies about his bride-to-be would be hard to bear and she feared he was about to confide in her. He said:

'You've never believed I was, have you?'

'Well, not exactly,' she prevaricated, for she could not apply the word love to the lust, desire, whatever Alex had shown towards her cousin. Love was giving of more than material things, which cost Alex nothing. Lovers should be humble, but Alex was incapable of humility. He had made his admission in a spirit of defiant resentment, despising his own weakness.

'Your feelings have changed?' She raised her eyes, very blue and serious, to his face.

'Yes ... no ... Oh, Jan!' He moved swiftly towards her and sitting down beside her again, seized her hand. Now it's coming, she thought, for his eyes were glowing and his face was alive with emotion, a description of Renata's perfections which she knew by heart, an outpouring of his newly developed devotion. There were limits to what she could bear and she tried to draw her hand away, faintly protesting: 'Please, Alex, don't!'

He did not relinquish it and, disturbed by something she could not define in his expression, she went on hurriedly, saying whatever came into her head.

'I've always felt you and Rena were made for each other. You make such an impressive pair, as if you were destined to come together ...' She faltered, for his eyes had started to smoulder and his hand tightened upon hers in a painful grip. 'In this part of the world everyone believes in fate,' she continued desperately, 'so of course you had to come to love her in the end.'

Her voice faded as she became aware of the tenseness of his attitude, as if he were restraining himself with great difficulty. Her fatuous remarks had been a blunder and he was annoyed by them.

'I . . . I suppose I was talking drivel,' she murmured.

'You were.'

'I'm sorry.' Her hand was growing numb in his grip. 'It's only that I'm so pleased about you and Rena. And I feel honoured to receive your confidence. You do think of me as a friend, don't you?'

'Nothing of the sort,' he said harshly, and threw away her hand. She rubbed it against her skirt to restore the circulation, and he made no apology for his brutality.

'The last thing I want is to be your friend!' He almost spat out the offending word.

'Oh!' She felt wounded by this rejection of her overture. 'You don't care for women friends?'

'There's only one possible relationship with a woman,' he told her cynically.

'I . . . I understand.' But she did not, when he had claimed her as a cousin he had been gentle, almost tender, now he seemed to be repudiating her. A possible explanation of his antagonism occurred to her. Naturally now he realised he cared for Renata he wanted to forget any previous backslidings.

'Perhaps because you . . . flirted with me,' she began awkwardly, 'you think I may want to make trouble between you and Rena. I'd never dream of doing such a thing. I know it was only because you were bored and lonely and she had offended you . . .'

He gave a startled exclamation, but she went on steadily:

'It was so, wasn't it? But we were neither of us in the least serious, it was what the French say, *pour passer les temps*. As I said before, a bit of ... fun.'

Alex caught her by the shoulders and stared down into her face with an enigmatical expression.

'Do you honestly mean to tell me that that is all it was to you?'

Jan summoned all her pride to her aid and met his gaze unflinchingly.

'Of course it was.' She forced a smile. 'I was just gaining a little ... experience, and you know what my opinion of you has always been, but I'm very glad to discover that with regard to Rena you're capable of ordinary human feelings.'

He pushed her away from him as if stung.

'You regard me as a sort of inhuman monster?'

'Oh, no, no!' she cried, distressed he should so interpret her words. 'You're only a little ... callous at times, but I don't understand why, if you're in love with Rena, you aren't engaged.'

'Because there's another woman whom I like and admire besides desiring her, who won't bore me to death after six months.'

'Oh, you're impossible!' Jan exclaimed, shocked and disappointed by this revelation. 'I don't believe such a woman exists.'

'She does, and until I'm convinced she's unattainable, I'm not going to accept second best. It is necessary that I should wed, and if my love continues to reject me, Renata will have to do.'

Jan stared at him wide-eyed, overwhelmed with re-

newed consternation. She had never suspected a prior
attachment, Alex's attentions to Renata had contra-
dicted such a possibility. His duplicity shocked her,
though if he were smarting from rejected love it might
account for his contempt for more susceptible women.
But there was something here which seemed off key.
Alex in the role of unsuccessful lover was uncharacter-
istic. She glanced at his dark arrogant face, the forceful jut of his chin. He was not a man who would admit
defeat in love or anything else. He had brought Renata
running after him in spite of her momentary panic, she
herself was at his feet, though mercifully he did not
know it. Yet why cook up such an unlikely story for
no apparent reason? But she could no longer suppose
that he loved Renata, and that he should callously use
her as a second string when whatever intrigue he was
involved in failed roused her to a pitch of angry indignation in her cousin's defence.

'You double-faced cur!' she blazed, her eyes flashing
blue fire. 'How dare you play with poor Rena when
your affections are engaged elsewhere! But who is this
lady-love of yours ... didn't she mind your long
absence in Kusadasi? Doesn't she resent your pursuit
of Rena?'

Alex smiled sardonically: 'I tried to make her
jealous.'

'Oh, you're an unscrupulous heel!' Jan cried vehemently. 'And to cap it all you've the effrontery to tell
me that you're in love, not with Rena, but someone
else. Did you expect me to sympathise with you?
You're a beast, a pig, a sadist, all the things I called you,
and I thought ...' She checked herself, on the verge of
tears. First impressions were often right; she had been

deceiving herself to imagine Alex had a softer side.

'You thought... what?' he asked, as if it were important to him.

'Oh, nothing, but this other woman must have some sense, she knows what you are. I hope she continues to spurn you, gives you hell. When I think how you've misled Rena I ... I could kill you!'

She raised her clenched fists as if she were about to strike him, and he caught her wrists in a firm grip.

'Calm down, spitfire. Hasn't Renata disillusioned you yet? Was she grateful to you for the heroic voyage you took upon her behalf?'

There was derision in his eyes and Jan wilted, recalling Renata's spiteful attack which he had foretold. The fire went out of her. It seemed she was doomed to bestow her love upon unworthy objects. Both Renata and Alex had shown up in a poor light. She gave a long sigh.

'Let me go, Alex. I'm sorry I abused you. You can't help being what you are, you've always warned me not to expect too much of you.'

Yet for all his faults and however despicably he behaved, she knew she could never wholly eradicate his image from her heart. He had captured her imagination, got under her skin, and even now, deploring his morals, hating him for Renata's sake, she was fighting an intense desire to throw herself into his arms.

He did not free her, though his clasp of her wrists loosened. The touch of his long, beautiful hands disturbed her against her will, and she drooped in his hold like a broken flower.

'Do you want me to marry Renata, though you know my heart is bestowed elsewhere?' he asked slowly.

'Having led her on, you certainly should,' she said firmly. 'And I don't think your heart would trouble you long. It seems to be a fairly adjustable organ.'

Alex blinked.

'What an indictment! And you, you have no qualms, no regrets?'

Jan frowned in puzzled bewilderment.

'No, of course not. I care nothing for you, but I pray you won't let Rena down.'

Alex dropped her wrists and stood up.

'If you change your mind, you've only yourself to blame,' he said cryptically, and walked away from her into the house without a backward look.

Jan watched him go with troubled eyes, not sure that he intended to stick to Renata, and in what way could it concern her? He seemed to be trying to make her responsible for a decision that was his alone. She speculated upon the mysterious woman whom he said he loved. If she did exist, and she was still doubtful about that, she must be some proud Athenian beauty, who disdained him for his mixed blood and business connections. She shrewdly suspected her attraction was because she was unattainable, and quite possibly if she relented, Alex would lose interest in her. But why had he confided in her? Perhaps because her importunities with regard to her cousin had annoyed him, and her mistake about the object of his love had irritated him. He had meant to shock her and had succeeded.

But had she done right by pressing Renata's claims? Could her cousin be happy with such a man? On the other hand, Renata's pride would suffer if Alex repudiated her now, so much so that she might become soured and embittered. Better an unloving husband than such a wound to her ego, and ... Jan smiled wryly ... she would be compensated by his gifts and jewels.

As for herself, Jan sighed again, she had wanted to believe the best of Alex. The Stephanos incident had raised him in her opinion, but where women were concerned he was untrustworthy. He must have forgotten the episode on deck in Istanbul harbour. He had not remembered his inamorata when he kissed her then, nor had he shrunk from the prospect of bedding her. It seemed his love was divorced from fidelity, and would such straying distress Renata? Should she warn her? But she knew Renata would not accept warnings from her and she would insist that any advances from Alex towards herself existed only in her imagination. There was nothing further she could do now. Her initial attempt to save Renata from Alex had resulted in leaving her with a sore heart, and from henceforth their destinies were outside her ken. Once back in England, she would do her best to forget all that happened in the Middle East.

At dinner that night, Mrs Leandris told her that arrangements had been made for her departure on the morrow. She was to meet Jeremy and Renata at the airport, whence they would fly back to England.

'Rena too?' Jan asked doubtfully, wondering what had happened.

'But of course, why should she stay here?' Lydia gave her guest a keen look. 'Alex will be following shortly,' she said. 'He has business in London.'

Jan gave a sigh of relief; the business was of course her cousin. She made a resolution that before he turned up in her uncle's house, she would be out of it. She was wearing her red dress, which fitted where it touched, with her hair drawn severely back. She had no colour in her cheeks and she looked like a pale ghost of the girl she had been on the night of her arrival. Lydia was studying her with disapproval.

'What has become of the pretty green dress?' she asked.

'Oh, I gave it to Rena,' Jan said offhandedly. 'She's a green chiffon girl, which I'm not, it was more suited to her.'

'But Alex gave it to you.'

'He lent it to me. I can't accept clothes from a man who is practically a stranger.'

Lydia seemed about to protest, but checked herself. She continued to eye Jan with disfavour. Presently she said:

'Your departure is a little sudden, but apparently Miss Reynolds is anxious to get home. You had a long talk with my son this morning. Did he mention it?'

Jan shook her head. She was fairly certain no arrangements had been made that morning. Alex must have decided he had had enough of her, and possibly their conversation had goaded him into action. Renata wanted to be married in London and would be eager to start preparations. Since Lydia had been absent, Alex must have told her about their 'long talk.'

'Mr Leandris seemed to be at a loose end this morning,' she said, to account for it.

'I hoped you would reach a ... er ... better understanding.'

Jan flushed uneasily. What was her hostess getting at?

'Believe me, Mrs Leandris, I understand your son very well,' she said coolly.

'Do you?' Lydia's gaze was searching. 'Alex is much more sensitive than many give him credit for. He had an unfortunate experience when he was much younger with a girl who turned out to be a mercenary coquette without a heart. It embittered him—we take disillusionment hard when we're young. Since then he's been a bit wild, motivated unconsciously by a desire to revenge himself on womankind, but now, at last, he's prepared to take a wife, and though you may not believe it, he'll make a good husband. He's had enough of light loving and what he wants, and needs, is a peaceful domestic life and, of course, children.'

'You should know,' Jan told her, feeling a knife in her wound. She did not think Renata wanted a peaceful, domestic life, and she had stipulated one child. She herself would have given him such homely pleasures, but she had never been in the running. She wondered if Lydia really knew her son as well as she thought she did, or if she was only voicing what she wanted for him. Alex himself might have very different ideas.

'I do know, and I thought he'd chosen wisely, but...'

She broke off and fiddled with her cutlery, seeming at a loss how to go on. Jan felt a little uncomfortable; Renata was not the sort of wife Lydia was envisioning, and it seemed she was having doubts. Apparently she knew nothing about the other woman, after whom Alex was still dangling.

'I'm sure Mr Leandris knows what he's doing,' she said vaguely.

'But do *you*?'

'Me?' Jan's eyes widened in surprise. 'What's it got to do with me?' Lydia gave an impatient exclamation, and she went on earnestly:

'I wish your son every happiness, Mrs Leandris, but I'll have little to do with him in future, as I'll be leaving home. Our ways lie far apart, as we decided this morning.'

'So I was told,' Lydia sighed. 'But you'll make him welcome when he arrives in London?'

'I'm sure we'll all do that,' Jan replied, 'but is it quite definite that he's coming?'

For if he were, it meant he would have relinquished all hope of winning that mysterious Athenian lady, who she was still inclined to believe was a myth, and Renata's prospects would be safe.

'Such is his intention. Alex is very persistent,' Lydia said significantly, thereby perplexing Jan all the more. Alex would be determined in pursuit, but by his own admission Renata was not the object of his desires, and since she was already won, why the need for persistence? Her resolution to be absent when he came strengthened.

To her relief Lydia dropped the subject of Alex, and began to discuss the details of her journey.

They parted next morning with polite thanks on the guest's part, and good wishes from the hostess.

'Perhaps we'll be seeing you back in Istanbul before long,' Mrs Leandris concluded.

'It's a fascinating city,' Jan said noncommittally. 'I hope I do see it again some time.'

She knew it was most unlikely and her hope was insincere. It would be redolent with memories of Alex and him she must forget. She climbed into the waiting taxi, waved to her hostess and was borne away from the house by the Bosphorus.

CHAPTER NINE

JAN had feared that Renata would be disappointed that she had not obtained her engagement ring, for she was not wearing one, and would vent some of her spleen on her, but her cousin seemed to belatedly realise that she had been less than fair to Jan, and set herself out to be charming. She talked gaily about Alex's arrival in London, so that Jan decided they must have a secret understanding, and she implied that he would purchase the ring then.

He did not come to the airport to see them off; he was engaged upon some important deal and could not spare the time, Renata told her, and she did not seem at all put out by this neglect. Her complacent attitude allayed Jan's doubts about the marriage. It was obvious Renata was not in love with Alex and would settle happily into what would be a marriage of convenience for the sake of the wealth and position it would give her.

As for Alex, he too seemed to have accepted the situation and was resigned to marrying Renata. He could accept defeat when expedient, though it was possible he had not given up hope of winning his inamorata, though he could no longer offer her a legal alliance, but for all she knew the woman might be already married.

She was troubled by the question he had asked her, whether he was lovable. It seemed to betray a secret doubt and a yearning. Though it was too coy a word to apply to her conception of the man, proud, dominant and arrogant, it did suggest that he needed love, real undemanding love, as she knew she herself could have given him if her feelings had a chance to develop, but Renata was incapable of such an emotion. Nor would he expect it of her, and Jan supposed she would suit him very well. Alex, like many another, sighed for the unattainable, but if he won it he would cease to desire it. Jan was advancing quickly in worldly wisdom; Alex had been an education.

Arrived home, Mrs Reynolds detached herself from her manifold clubs and guilds sufficiently to give them a welcome. Remarking that Renata was blooming and Jan looked washed out, she absently embraced her husband and retired to her writing desk. She too was proud of her daughter's beauty, but they had never been close. Ruth Reynolds was a reserved woman and neither Renata nor Jan had ever penetrated her absorption in her good works. Perhaps she had some excuse to seek an antidote, for Jeremy had soon after the honeymoon betrayed that he found heathen goddesses much more exciting than mere wives. His present to her of another effigy of the 'Diana of the Ephesians', similar but bigger and better than the one Alex had given Renata, was given only perfunctory thanks.

On the next morning Jan went to a hairdresser and had her hair cut and waved. The transformation in her appearance pleased her. Curling softly round her face, the style suited her and made her look more alert and modern. The severed clippings on the floor were the discard of her former self, the girl Alex had mocked and derided.

The following day she went to an agency and was immediately offered a temporary position as holiday relief in a big city firm. She accepted it, it would be a start, and set about finding accommodation, which was more difficult. Eventually she obtained a room in a hostel, but that was only temporary too, though it would give her time to locate the bed-sitting-room which was what she really wanted. She had achieved her main object, to be out of the house when Alex arrived.

Renata sympathised with her endeavours.

'No life for you here when I'm gone,' she said. 'You're sensible to get out.' She regarded her cousin critically. 'You've improved in looks since we've been away, and I like your hair.'

In addition to her hair-cut, Jan had bought herself a well-fitting linen two-piece, as the weather was still warm, though she was not yet using make-up.

'Since I shan't be in your shadow any longer it's worth while making the best of myself,' she returned.

Renata looked smug. 'I suppose it has been a bit hard on you, being contrasted with me all the time, but I appreciate what a good friend you've always been to me. I shan't forget you when I'm married. You must spend your holidays with me.'

Jan thanked her and was cheered by her cousin's tardy praise, but did not say that holidays with the Leandris family were definitely out. Renata would probably forget all about her invitation when she was caught up in her husband's social life.

Jeremy grumbled about Jan's desertion but accepted

the part-time typist she found for him, and was soon unaware of any change. Her aunt did not seem to notice her absence.

Jan was working in the typing pool of a big multiple food buying concern, and since her work gave satisfaction there was every prospect of being permanently employed when the holiday period was over, but it was soul-deadening work and she resolved she must find something better when she had proved her efficiency. Both at the office and in the hostel she was mixing with young people of her own age, but they seemed shallow and frivolous to her, while the young men she encountered appeared to belong to a different species from Alex. He had spoilt her for all ordinary contacts. Since she was unable to wholly disguise her disdain she was labelled snooty and stand-offish, which she did not deserve. She was willing to be friendly, but could find no common interest with her associates.

At first during the process of adapting herself to her new life, she had little time to repine for Alex, nor did she often visit her home, but from occasional phone calls she ascertained that he had not put in an appearance. This seemed ominous, and she began to wonder if he had decided to wash out the Reynolds family, or if his Athenian lady had relented. If the latter were the case, then Renata's hopes were doomed. Not that she seemed to be much concerned. Jan met her in the cloakroom belonging to a small restaurant where she sometimes went for a meal in the evening when she had been working late and would miss the hostel dinner. Renata was looking more beautiful than ever, exuding a soft glow so that Jan felt sure Alex must have arrived.

She seemed a little disconcerted to see Jan.

'I didn't know this was a haunt of yours,' she remarked.

'I don't come here often, funds don't allow,' Jan told her. 'Are you alone?'

It was a very ordinary restaurant and a place where Alex would scorn to entertain a girl-friend.

'I'm with a friend,' Renata hesitated, then decided to be candid. 'An old acquaintance,' she went on. 'You've met him.'

'Him?' Jan looked her question.

'Denis Wood,' Renata told her. 'And you needn't look so shocked. I'm not engaged yet and at the rate things are going, I never shall be. Alex seems to have forgotten me.'

'You've not been back very long, and you know how tied up with business he always seems to be,' Jan tried to reassure her, while feeling considerably disquieted.

'I'm more important than his stuffy old business,' Renata declared peevishly, while she touched up her make-up. She glanced round to see if anyone was listening, but no one was in their immediate vicinity. It was a large cloakroom with a row of wash basins, the place being a popular rendezvous. Jan was tidying her hair in the mirror next to her.

'That short style suits you,' she observed absently, then dropping her voice: 'I don't know what happened on that trip of yours, but he's never been the same since.'

'Nothing happened.' Jan concentrated upon arranging her hair. 'But he found it difficult to forgive you for letting him down.'

'Not allowing him to seduce me,' Renata snapped. 'I've got some sense, Jan, and you see my refusal brought him up to scratch in the end.' She looked disconsolately at her left hand. 'But he might have given me a ring.'

'Then he did actually propose?'

'In a roundabout way.' She glanced narrowly at her cousin. 'Did he ever confide in you?'

'Can you see Mr Leandris pouring his heart out to a stowaway?' Jan enquired lightly, for she must never betray to Renata the existence of that other woman, which she hoped she would never discover.

'No, he always regarded you as something between a half-wit and an unfledged adolescent,' Renata told her cheerfully. 'No offence, Jan, but you knew that.'

'Yes, I did.' But he had not done so on that night in Istanbul. She put her comb in her handbag. 'It's been nice to see you, Rena, but won't Denis be wondering where you are?'

'Oh, he knows I always spend hours titivating,' Renata dismissed his possible impatience. 'You won't tell anyone I went out with him?' she added anxiously.

Jan knew anyone meant Alex.

'I'm no tell-tale,' she declared, 'but are you wise? If Alex did get to know, he might be nasty. Greeks are very jealous.'

'Then he should come and assert his claims,' Renata decided. 'I wouldn't be surprised if he isn't having a final flutter before getting married, so he's no right to object to Denis.'

Jan feared she was right. There could only be one explanation for Alex's tardiness; he was making a last appeal to the woman he said he loved. Perhaps it

would be better for Renata if he did jilt her, for she
was sure she was marrying the wrong man.

'Rena,' she began earnestly, 'give him up, he isn't
worthy of you. Money isn't everything, and you do love
Denis, don't you?'

'Ssh!' Renata glanced round. Several women had
entered in a laughing group. Under cover of their
chatter, she almost hissed:

'That would suit you, wouldn't it? I'm not blind,
Jan, but even if I ditched him, he'd never look at you.'
The green eyes were venomous, and Jan wished she
would not reiterate the obvious. Much of her lack of
self-confidence was due to her cousin's denigration.

Renata went on more normally: 'I've told you before I can't live on a shoe-string, and things have
gone too far now. I wouldn't want to break Alex's
heart.'

Jan nearly said, 'Who are you trying to kid?' but
restrained herself. Renata was adept at self-deception
where her vanity was concerned, but Alex's heart was
no more involved than Renata's was. She did not want
to be questioned about that, and their companions were
throwing curious glances at them. It was a blow to discover that Renata suspected her own feelings towards
Alex, but they would not be having much contact in
future. Renata picked up her handbag with a careless,
'So long, Jan,' and stalked out of the cloakroom.

Following more slowly Jan saw her seated in a
corner with Denis gazing adoringly into her face. She
pitied them both, Renata for her lack of courage, Denis
for his hopeless love. With a little contriving, surely
they could manage? Denis was not a pauper, he looked
well dressed and well groomed, and Jeremy could be

persuaded to give Renata an allowance until he was earning more. But both father and daughter were caught in Alex's glittering net. His affluence and personality blinded them, and they could not bear to dissociate themselves from him, though he could bring them nothing but unhappiness, as he had to her.

Two days later Alexandros Leandris arrived in London. He was sufficiently important for his advent to be mentioned by the press. Jan inadvertently witnessed it on television. She was in the general sitting room at the hostel when the news was shown, and saw a close-up of his distinguished figure being accosted by an importunate reporter.

'There is a rumour, Mr Leandris, that your reason for coming to London is a romantic one.'

She recognised his familiar sardonic smile as he replied:

'You fellows would scent romance in an office file. My visit is purely upon business.'

'Can you tell us what business, sir?'

'No, it's confidential.'

The announcer made a reference to shipping tycoons, and that was all, but Jan's heart was fluttering and the palms of her hands were damp. She certainly must keep out of his way, but that would not be difficult, as there was no reason whatever why they should meet.

'Striking looking guy,' one of the girls commented. 'But I suppose he's married, the best lookers always are.'

'They don't always stay married,' another one pointed out. 'Evidently there's been some gossip or the chap wouldn't have mentioned it.'

The first speaker sighed. 'No chance of him coming within our orbit,' she said mournfully. 'He isn't for the likes of us.'

Nor me, either, Jan thought, and wondered what the girls would say if she told them she had spent three days aboard his yacht. They would think she was making it up, and in that ordinary room it did seem like a fantasy that had never really occurred. She wished she had not seen the picture; she had been trying to put him out of her life, but the sight of his familiar features had awoken her longing for his presence, the touch of his hand, the sound of his voice. Useless to insist he was a reprobate, unworthy of her love, and Renata's future husband; she would give—well, nearly anything to be in his arms again. Renata had scornfully described her as something between a half-wit and an unfledged adolescent. That might have been Alex's first impression of her, but in the end he had become almost a friend. But it was not his friendship she wanted and he had told her he did not want women friends. He had kissed her, and as if he had meant it ... at the time. That was a memory she would carry to her grave. Like Sir Andrew Aguecheek, she had been adored once, if only for a moment, though love was hardly the right word for what had motivated Alex. In this mood of sad reminiscence she went to bed and woke to the realisation that Alex was actually in the same town where she worked and lived, but London was vast and he was as remote from her as if he were still in Turkey.

Next day something occurred to divert her thoughts. She was advised by post that an agency to which she had applied had found her a vacant bed-sitting-room and she could take up residence at once. The hostel, having a long waiting list, was willing to release her, so she was able to move in at once. It was not much of a place, being situated in a terrace of old houses near Swiss Cottage, but it was central and it was hers without anybody to interfere with her. So alienated was she from her family that she did not bother to advise them of her new address; she would get round to it some time. For the first week she came back to it each evening with a feeling of satisfaction, she had her own pad, a place where she could do exactly as she pleased without criticism or objection, but her elation was succeeded by dejection. She was quite alone.

She found the long hours of regular work tiring, for the summer abroad had sapped her not very great reserves of strength and she lacked the energy to go out to seek new contacts at clubs or recreation centres. She fell into the habit of dreaming her evenings away after she had done her few chores. There were two armchairs on either side of the gas fire with which she had been provided, and she would imagine the one opposite to hers was occupied by a man—a man with the face and form of Alex but an entirely different disposition. Kind where Alex was cruel, loving while Alex was indifferent, a friend and not an enemy. The fantasy was weakness for which she at times despised herself. It would fade when she found other interests, but as yet she had no will to do so. He would never come to her humble room and she was not doing anybody any harm by creating his image there.

To her relief, Renata had not suggested that she should be her bridesmaid, and by avoiding her uncle's house she was spared all discussion of the wedding. Renata would want an impressive affair with all the trimmings, and she would make a most glamorous bride. She would choose for her attendants girls who would be an adornment to the spectacle, which Jan would only mar. If Alex produced any representatives from his family, they would be as decorative as himself, and she was thankful for her cousin's neglect. Any suggestion that she should be included made by her aunt and uncle would be overruled, and her nonappearance at home would show her lack of interest. Alex, she was sure would prefer that she was not present, but that was making herself too important. He would allow Renata to have her way in arranging a ceremony which Jan suspected he would consider a bore, and not even notice that Jan had not been included.

For all that she had a strange feeling of expectancy that she would one day meet him in the streets or on the tube, though she knew it was most unlikely that she should do so, for her environment was not his. He would go everywhere by taxi and the expensive hotels and restaurants would be his haunts.

She tried to assure herself that the last thing she wanted to do was to run into him, and what she felt was dread at the possibility, but the sense of expectancy ... it was not dread ... persisted.

She would be glad when it was all over and he and Renata left for Greece and there was no chance of a meeting, however unlikely that chance might be.

Modern London is not without its hazards, and returning one night to Camden Town, where she changed from the tube to a bus, she was dismayed to discover some sort of riot seemed to be in progress. A clash between rival demonstrators had resulted in a milling mob, and she stood for a while at the entrance to the station wondering if it would be wiser to go back underground. But she had been working late and wanted to get home, and there was no reason why anyone should molest her. So she sought to push her way towards where her bus should be waiting, but there was no bus. Deciding she would walk, she turned about and found her way barred by an evil-looking lout.

'Got any dough on you, chick?'

She backed away as he snatched at her handbag, clutching it to her breast. She had not much money on her, but it contained her keys and other useful articles. The man grabbed at her wrist.

'C'mon, give it over.'

'Get out of my way! I'll call the police.'

'P'lice 'ave got other things to do. I don't want to get rough. No one ain't going to 'elp you in this scrum.'

But there he was wrong. A brown fist caught him between the eyes, and as he fell, Jan's waist was encircled by a strong arm and she was whisked away into a waiting taxi. Some stones were thrown at them as it moved away, the driver pursuing an erratic course through the crowd which gave way reluctantly before them. He turned into a comparatively quiet side street and drove fast for a while until the mob was outdistanced.

Jan had been badly shaken by the menacing crowd and the attempted robbery, but she was overwhelmed by Alex's swift and unexpected rescue. She clung to him as he held her on the back seat of the taxi, while the tears poured down her cheeks. He cradled her as if she were a hurt child, enquiring anxiously:

'Did that brute harm you?' And as she murmured something inarticulate: 'Jan, Jan, little one, don't cry like that!'

'I ... I can't ... help it,' she sobbed. 'Oh, Alex, Alex, I've wanted you so!'

All her defences were down, her brave efforts to conceal her feelings blown away like chaff before the wind. Miraculously Alex had come to her, how and whence she had no idea, but he was here, she was in his arms, and far from being mocking or deriding her, he was being ... kind. Vaguely in her confused state, she identified him with the fantasy image that she had created to assuage her loneliness. None of this could be really happening, it was a dream.

Somewhere in the region of Regents Park, the driver slowed down and pushed back the dividing panel.

'All clear now, sir. Where to next?'

'Where do you live, Jan?'

Mechanically she gave her address. She must be having a delusion. Alex was taking her back to her room, he would sit in the armchair as she had so often pictured him and then he would ... vanish. She clung to him, desperately fearful of losing him.

'Don't leave me, don't ever leave me!'

'Certainly I shan't, not after this touching demonstration, so there's no need to strangle me.'

This was the Alex she knew, so he must be real. With an effort she managed to regain her self-control and drawing away from him, fumbled in her handbag for a handkerchief. Anticipating her need, he produced his own much larger one and wiped her eyes himself.

'Better now?'

'Yes, but—Oh, Alex, what must you think of me!'

'That I'll tell you in due course.'

'I . . . I was upset . . .'

'Never mind that now. It was lucky I was passing. I saw you come out of the station and lost you in the crowd, then I sighted you again with that scum.'

'But what on earth were you doing in Camden Town?'

'Looking for you. Renata told me where you were staying, but they said you had left. The directions they gave me were a bit vague. You shouldn't be living on your own.'

His tone was elder-brotherly, admonishing. Her uncle must have expressed belated concern about her and had asked him to locate her; guiltily she recalled that she had not communicated with her family for some time.

The taxi halted in front of the building where she lodged. Alex sprang out and turned to hand her out. Reluctantly she left the shelter of the cab. For a brief spell it seemed as if a miracle had occurred and he had been seeking her, but she had arrived at a more prosaic explanation. Jeremy had sent him and nothing was changed.

She rummaged in her bag for her latch key while Alex paid the taxi-driver. He was a burly, phlegmatic character, who had run a considerable risk while he waited for his fare to do his rescue act. That Alex appreciated that was expressed in the bundle of notes he passed to him. Jan had mounted the short flight of steps leading to the front door which was ajar when he joined her. His mission must include ascertaining in what sort of place she was living, but she was reluctant to introduce him to her room. It was bound to appear poor and mean to his critical eyes.

Evening sunlight relieved the drabness of the street, but it was a far cry from the house by the Bosphorus. Alex was wearing one of his light grey business suits, perfectly cut, and as usual appeared immaculate, he looked like a being from another planet.

'Well?' he demanded. 'Aren't you going to ask me in?'

'I ... I've only got a bed-sit.'

'Male visitors not permitted?'

'There's no embargo on them.'

'Then why are you prevaricating? I've often wondered what comprised a bed-sit. Your uncle seems to think you're living in a slum. We can't talk in the street.'

So Jeremy *had* sent him; she prayed he was not going to ask her to his wedding.

'It's not as bad as that,' she said, and led the way up the stairs to the first floor where her room was situated. She unlocked the door and ushered him in.

'Sit down,' she indicated the armchair in which she had so often visualised him. 'Would you like some coffee? It's only instant, I'm afraid, I have most of my meals out, and I'm only at home in the evenings. I'll put the kettle on.'

She went behind the screen which concealed the sink, gas ring and her few culinary effects, taking the opportunity to wash her face, which still felt tear-stained. The act of making the coffee restored her to her normal composure. When she returned carrying the two steaming cups, Alex was prowling round the room looking at its simple furnishings. It really did not look too bad, she thought, for it was fitted with bright curtains and covers, cushions disguising the divan bed, and there was a vase of flowers on the table. At her reappearance he sat down again in the armchair, and she placed the cup beside him thinking how handsome and distinguished he looked and how out of place. She said defensively:

'I can hardly expect you to appreciate my room, but it's the first time I've had a place of my own and there are plenty worse.'

'I don't doubt it.' Absently he stirred his cup, studying her closely over its rim, and Jan flushed under his quizzical gaze.

'So you've cut it off.'

She had forgotten about her changed coiffure, and she touched her curls self-consciously.

'Don't you think it's an improvement?'

'No, I liked your hair. Presumably it would grow again?'

'If I let it, but I shan't.'

She had sat down opposite to him, and she sipped her coffee, but tasted nothing. Alex did, and made a grimace.

'So this is Janet Reynolds, the career girl,' he commented. 'Bed-sit, instant coffee ... are you happy?'

Her eyes dropped before his penetrating gaze.

'It's what I wanted to do.'

'Why can you never answer a question directly?' he complained.

'I'm happy to be independent,' she assured him. 'I don't have to please anybody except myself.'

'But aren't you lonely?'

She looked away. That was the flaw in her new freedom.

'It's early days yet,' she explained. 'Later on I expect I'll make lots of friends. It's only a matter of time.'

'But you won't have any time,' he almost purred. 'After your performance in the taxi, you don't imagine I'm going to let you stay here?'

She stared at him blankly.

'Alex, are you mad? Of course I'm staying here, whatever anyone says. You've come to England to marry Renata ...'

'That I'm not.'

'Oh no!' She was appalled. 'You can't back out now.'

'I haven't backed out as you so elegantly put it. Renata has done the backing. She has found she prefers Denis Wood.'

CHAPTER TEN

JAN'S first thought was that Renata had been crazily indiscreet. Someone must have recognised her on one of her secret meetings with Denis and reported it. She knew that as far as she could love anyone except herself, Renata was in love with Denis Wood. Unlike Alex, he never opposed her wishes, and his uncritical adoration flattered her, but she had always insisted she could not afford to marry a comparatively poor man.

Naturally Alex would not stand for such competition, though he had no scruples about two-timing himself. He had always been contemptuous of poor

Denis, not believing he could ever be a serious rival and would have been furious to discover Renata's deception which was no compliment to himself. He had every right to be angry, for he had come to England as an expectant bridegroom, and found his bride was going out with another man. She would not put it past him to use physical violence on the delinquent pair.

Having delivered his bombshell, Alex became silent, watching her covertly through half-closed lids. Finally she said stupidly:

'So there'll be no wedding?'

'On the contrary, there'll be two, though not a double one.'

'Two?' Jan knitted her brows in perplexity. 'Which of you is going to marry Rena?'

'Denis Wood, of course.' Alex laughed good-humouredly. 'Your cousin is adept at staging surprises. I called at the house unexpectedly, having arrived a day earlier than scheduled, and your aunt ushered me into a room where they were both canoodling on the sofa, whereat she promptly disappeared. Renata was profuse with excuses, but young Wood spoke up like a man. He accused me of corrupting Renata with my wealth and power, declaring she had been the sweetest girl who ever walked ... God, the fellow must be infatuated! So I asked him if he'd like to learn how such wealth was obtained, at which your charming cousin pricked up her ears. The upshot was, I was cajoled into taking him into my employ at a salary he's not worth, though he may be in a few years, and since he will be able to keep her—well, not in the style I could have done, but near enough, they are going to marry.'

Jan was astonished by this recital, delivered half-humorously, half deprecatingly. Instead of venting his rage upon the couple, Alex was actually going to help them. It showed, as she had often suspected, he was not nearly as hard-hearted as he liked to appear, but to give up Renata so tamely indicated that he was no longer interested in her, which she could not credit. She ejaculated feebly:

'Don't you mind?'

'Why should I? I've always known Renata was only attracted to me by my affluence. She regarded me as a sort of ogre who had to be endured to satisfy her greed.'

This, Jan knew, had been partly true, but when her cousin had told her preparations for her wedding were in train, she had hoped Renata had come to have some regard for her intended spouse.

'But ... but you'd promised to marry her,' she protested. 'That's why she came to Istanbul.'

'It was not. How you and she interpreted my suggestion that she and her father returned home via Istanbul into an offer of marriage is beyond my comprehension. I would never marry Renata, I told you that back in Kusadasi, or I told her, I'm not sure which, but I didn't mind having an affair if that was what she wanted, and I was quite prepared to pay handsomely for her favours. Possibly she showed you an emerald and diamond pendant which was an instalment in advance.'

Jan nodded unhappily, for this was an aspect of Alex which she abhorred. All the epithets she had hurled at him at that time were deserved, except that she had learned to take a more tolerant view of such liaisons.

A virile man of the world like he was could not be expected to live like a monk, and they were a common occurrence nowadays. Renata's heart had not been involved and apparently he had not made her any false promises.

To change a painful subject, she enquired:

'You mentioned two weddings. Does that mean that the lady you . . .' she swallowed, '. . . love has relented?'

'I'm confident she has.'

'Oh, then there'll be a happy ending for everybody.'

Except for herself, but she had never anticipated otherwise. The Athenian lady was a reality after all and now Alex had disposed of Renata, he would go back to Greece to claim her. What he had told the reporter was correct, he had come to England solely on business, and only good manners had caused him to call upon the Reynolds household. She did not know what had been going on there since she had left it, but it would seem Renata had deliberately misled her with her talk about the wedding. There had been no preparations, Renata had embroidered them; she had never forgiven Jan for going off with Alex, and had sought to establish a prior claim.

'I hope so,' Alex said gravely, in response to her remark. He leaned forward, looking at her intently.

'Why did you put on that act on the terrace that morning?' he asked gently. 'You deceived me completely, but was it necessary?'

Jan knew then that she must have betrayed herself completely in the taxi, though she could not recollect clearly what she had done and said in her agitation. She had wept, and he had held her in his arms, or she had thrown herself into them, but what was the use of further prevarication? She was not ashamed of her love, though it was not reciprocated, and before he left she would put everything straight between them.

Lifting her head proudly, she met his tawny eyes with complete candour in her blue gaze. A becoming flush stained her normally pale cheeks, and with her soft brown hair curling about her heart-shaped face, and her delicate features, she looked more than pretty. But of that she was completely unaware. In her own estimation she was a plain jane, and always would be.

'I have a little pride,' she said steadily. 'On that particular morning you were describing your feelings for someone else, and your intention of marrying Rena as second best, which rather contradicts your statement that you never would, unless you had an ulterior motive for making me believe so.'

Alex grinned. 'I too have some pride. I found the role of rejected lover humiliating.'

'Well, I didn't want to bolster your ego by admitting I'd fallen for you myself, but be that as it may,' she went on hastily as he seemed about to interrupt. 'And as we're unlikely to meet again I won't prevaricate any more. I do love you, Alex, and I'm not ashamed to confess it, but I ask nothing in return. I hope you'll be very happy and perhaps you'll think of me sometimes, because those days on the *Artemis* were the highlight of my life.'

'Ah!' Alex drew a long breath of satisfaction. 'At last! Come here, Jan.'

'Still the same Alex!' She smiled wanly. 'That wasn't an invitation, it was a valediction.'

'To hell with your long words!'

He sprang to his feet and reached for her hands,

pulling her to her feet. Holding them both in his, he stared down into her face with a flicker of flame in his eyes.

'I told you you were stupid and obtuse and you've been unbelievably slow. Oh, yes, I know, when you took Renata's place I was furious to have you foisted on to me, but you didn't cringe or ask for mercy. You began to intrigue me, you were so unlike any girl I'd ever known, and during the hours we spent together I found you companionable and amusing, totally without guile or avarice, and your loyalty to that unpleasant cousin of yours was praiseworthy. My liking for you grew into love, but you would not see what was happening, in fact you're a bull-headed, contumacious little idiot. Even though you responded to my kisses, you persisted in treating me as if I were some sort of predatory animal. I'm not that bad, Jan.'

'I know you're not, but I never dreamed...' She was unable to grasp what he was telling her, though his rudeness suggested he was sincere. 'You can't really mean what you're saying, you couldn't come to care for me, when you have the pick of lovely women. I'm so plain and insignificant...'

'Your piquant little face is more attractive to me than any painted beauty, and in that green dress you looked quite lovely, like a water nymph.'

Recollection stung, she snatched her hands away, crying bitterly:

'The dress you bought for Renata!'

'I did not. Those clothes were what I told you, spare parts for castaways. If she told you otherwise, she lied, and I don't think that's the only falsehood she perpetrated. Renata, my sweet, guessed what you were too blind to see and was madly jealous. Incidentally, I've made her give it up, I don't want anyone else to wear it.'

'I can't take it, I don't want it,' Jan said feverishly. She could not rid herself of the conviction that Alex was somehow making game of her. She was so conditioned to consider herself of no account, she could not accept that he who was a prince among men could really care for her humble self. She had been a fool to tell him she loved him, naturally he would take the opportunity to rib her.

'You've always enjoyed teasing me,' she went on, 'but what about the Athenian lady?'

It was his turn to look blank.

'What Athenian lady?'

'You never mentioned her name, so I've always thought of her as that. I mean the woman who resisted you for so long, but you say has capitulated. The woman ... you love.'

'Only one woman has resisted me, and I always meant to wear her down in the end. I'm a very persistent man, Jan, when I want something, so beware!' Then as recollection returned to him, he laughed. 'I'd clean forgotten my little bit of fiction which I invented to save my face when you snubbed me and threw Renata down my throat.'

So she had been a myth after all.

'When I want something, I don't give up,' Alex went on. 'That has been the recipe for my success. My mother told me that she was sure you cared for me and she thought Renata was the obstacle. She has been eliminated now, and when I grabbed you this evening, you greeted me rapturously.'

'Who wouldn't under such circumstances?' Jan said dryly. 'I was scared.'

She looked at him searchingly, still unable to credit that he meant what he had said. She had always considered herself a dud where men were concerned, and that Alex loved her was quite incredible. She shook her brown head in disbelief.

'You can't really want me, Alex, a plain ordinary girl like me, when you're so . . . so . . . magnificent.'

'Magnificent, am I? That's a nice change from pig, cad and sadist—you see I remember them all. Oh, don't be so humble, Jan! You're the one girl who wouldn't bore me to death after six months, and I've been courting you ever since you came on board my yacht. At Istanbul you melted in my arms, and I thought I'd won then, but no, as soon as Renata turned up you became an iceberg. I'm going to kiss you again and then perhaps it'll penetrate your thick skull that I love you, need you, and I won't be denied.'

He snatched her to him in a close embrace, and his lips sought hers. All her repressed longings surged to the surface as she responded to his demanding mouth. Her arms went round his neck, as she pressed herself against him. She became aware that Alex had moved towards the divan, and as he laid her down upon it, she knew a moment's panic, but it passed as quickly as it came. So let it be, she would have her hour of fulfilment, come what may. As once before, his hands moved caressingly over her body, unfastening her dress so that he could kiss her breasts, her clasp of his neck tightened as she sought to bring his head down upon them. Then to her hurt surprise she realised that he was withdrawing from her, and she murmured a faint protest.

He sat up, breathing fast, and mopped his forehead with his handkerchief. Then he smiled at her a little ruefully.

'We'll wait,' he said firmly. 'I must prove to you I'm not the lustful brute you've always insisted I am. It need not be for long. I can arrange for the marriage to take place at the Greek consulate, and ... what's the matter now?'

For Jan too had sat up, she was crouched against the cushions, pulling up her dress, staring at him with wide startled eyes.

'I couldn't marry you, Alex.'

'Oh, my God,' he exclaimed in exasperation, 'why ever not? What else did you think I meant?'

'But ... but it's impossible. You're an important man, you need a beautiful wife. You'd be ashamed to present me to your friends, your mother ...'

'Rubbish! She declares you're just the right woman for me, though I was sure of that myself. Will you stop playing hard to get?'

Jan remained mute, overwhelmed by the prospect before her.

Alex glanced contemptuously about the room.

'Don't you understand you'll finish with all this? I can give you wealth, and position ...'

'That's just it.' Her eyes were wide with dismay. 'I don't care for wealth, and I'd never be able to cope with your ... position. I'd disgrace you. If only you'd been poor!'

He laughed with genuine amusement.

'Believe me, it's only too easy to become used to

affluence. And don't tell me you can't cope with anything if you set your mind to it. Look what you've reduced me to, an importunate lover who swore I'd never trust a woman again.'

That diverted her.

'She let you down, didn't she?' she asked shyly. 'Your mother told me about her.'

'She'd no right to do that,' he said shortly. 'It's true, though. I believed she was an angel and she turned out to be a mercenary bitch. I wasn't so well off then and she found a higher bidder. It distorted my values and I scorned all women until I met you. Did it never occur to you that I wanted to marry you?'

'Good heavens, no!'

'But I asked you if you would marry me and you said certainly not.'

Jan recalled the sunlit terrace by the Bosphorus, the geraniums glowing scarlet, and Alex, mocking and derisive.

'I never imagined that was a serious proposal, and you were contracted to Rena.'

'Which I always denied, though you wouldn't believe me.'

'She's so beautiful,' Jan began.

'I've known many as good-looking, and most of them were soulless.' He moved impatiently. 'Damn it all, Jan, what else can I say to convince you? Do you love me or do you not?'

'I do, Alex,' she said earnestly, 'but so much so that I won't marry you. You want me now, but that's only because I've been, what was it you said? hard to get. But if we married, you'd come to see what a plain, homely creature I am, and when your friends sneered at . . . at your choice, you'd want to be rid of me.'

'You still seem to think I'm a despicable character,' he complained bitterly. 'None of that is true, and at one time you thought yourself vastly superior to my erring self, and so you are in some ways. You'll drive me crazy if you keep on denying me.'

'But I'm not. Did I deny you just now? I'm yours, Alex, to take if you wish.'

'No!' he exclaimed violently. 'I can't do that. You're a good woman, Jan, and I won't let you violate your finer feelings.'

A complete reversal had come about. She, who had once upbraided him for not respecting Renata's innocence, was prepared to surrender her own, and he had refused her offer.

Silence fell between them. Alex had sunk his head in his hands, and Jan changed her position so that she was sitting beside him. Suddenly he slipped down on his knees, encircling her waist with his arms, and laid his head on her lap.

'Jan, my little Jan,' he murmured softly, 'don't you understand, I want you always by my side. I need you, Jan, so much. I know I'm often hard and domineering, but if you'll marry me you can teach me to be a better man.'

This appeal moved her profoundly. For the first time she glimpsed the lonely man beneath his pride and arrogance, who craved, as we all do, to be loved. Gently she began to stroke his bent black head, marvelling that he who had always seemed so inaccessible had humbled himself to plead with her.

'That's a strong inducement, Alex,' she said with a

quiver of laughter in her voice, 'though I don't know that I want to change you.'

'You see, not only do I need a wife,' his voice was muffled against her skirt, 'but I want a family. Wouldn't you wish to have a child?'

Jan remembered Renata's recoil from motherhood and her own reaction. To bear Alex's son had been the height of her fantasies, and children would be a lasting bond between them.

'Oh, Alex!' she breathed, and there was assent in her voice. She bent down and cradled his head in her arms. He looked up at her with the familiar wicked glint in his eyes.

'We couldn't allow it to be a b... illegitimate, could we?'

'Of course not!' She was half laughing, half crying. 'So it'll have to be marriage, Alex.'

He raised himself with a hand on either side of her on the divan, and gazed deep into her eyes.

'It most certainly will, and I promise you I'll make sure you never regret it.'

They kissed again, long and lingeringly, but this time there was less of passion and more of tenderness. When they drew apart he said:

'And you'll grow your hair again?'

'Anything you say, my lord and master.'

He raised his eyebrows. 'Don't tell me you're going to be a submissive wife!'

'Isn't that what you want?'

He grinned. 'Not from you, you couldn't keep it up anyway. I once told you I didn't care for doormats.'

Jan's eyes sparkled mischievously. 'Yes, you said you would prefer a challenge to subdue.'

To her surprise he shook his head.

'Forget all that, Jan,' he said earnestly. 'There's no question of subduing or being subdued between you and me. You must be my partner and helpmate.'

This had always been Jan's view of marriage, but she had not expected Alex to share it.

'I fear I'll be a little inadequate in that role,' she said sadly.

'Rubbish! You *must* rid yourself of that inferiority complex. My darling girl, considering the awkward situations you've surmounted since first I met you, being my wife will be a sinecure. Now let me take you out to dinner to celebrate our engagement.'

All Jan's fears and apprehensions suddenly fell away, and she seemed to grow in stature as she took the hand he offered. She could not be so ineffective after all since she had won her love against overwhelming odds.

'I've always thought it would be very satisfactory to be a matriarch,' she told him gaily, 'one of those superior ladies everyone looks up to and secretly fears.'

'Plenty of time for that,' he returned. 'No doubt you'll become one eventually, but first we have to found a family, and to do that, you'll have to accept my co-operation.'

'I'm counting on that, Mr Leandris.'

Laughing, joking, they went out into the street, and the future stretched fair before them.

Distinctively Different

Harlequin Presents...

Beautiful love stories that offer
the excitement of exotic places,
warm, true-to-life characters,
and the thrill of romance.

Rare blends of sophistication,
refreshing realism and drama that
let your imagination sweep you into
the special world of love that only
Harlequin can create!

*From the publisher that understands
how you feel about love.*

Harlequin Presents...

Harlequin Romances

The books that let you escape
into the wonderful world of romance!
Trips to exotic places... interesting
plots... meeting memorable people...
the excitement of love.... These are
integral parts of Harlequin Romances —
the heartwarming novels read by
women everywhere.

Many early issues are now available.
Choose from this great selection!

Choose from this list of Harlequin Romance editions.*

*Some of these book were originally published under different titles.

Relive a great love story...
with Harlequin Romances
Complete and mail this coupon today!

Harlequin Reader Service

In U.S.A.
MPO Box 707
Niagara Falls, N.Y. 14302

In Canada
649 Ontario St.
Stratford, Ontario, N5A 6W2

Please send me the following Harlequin Romance novels. I am enclosing my check or money order for $1.25 for each novel ordered, plus 59¢ to cover postage and handling.

☐ 422	☐ 509	☐ 636	☐ 729	☐ 810	☐ 902
☐ 434	☐ 517	☐ 673	☐ 737	☐ 815	☐ 903
☐ 459	☐ 535	☐ 683	☐ 746	☐ 838	☐ 909
☐ 481	☐ 559	☐ 684	☐ 748	☐ 872	☐ 920
☐ 492	☐ 583	☐ 713	☐ 798	☐ 878	☐ 927
☐ 508	☐ 634	☐ 714	☐ 799	☐ 888	☐ 941

Number of novels checked @ $1.25 each = $_____

N.Y. and Ariz. residents add appropriate sales tax. $_____

Postage and handling $_____.59

TOTAL $_____

I enclose _____
(Please send check or money order. We cannot be responsible for cash sent through the mail.)

Prices subject to change without notice.

NAME _____
(Please Print)

ADDRESS _____

CITY _____

STATE/PROV. _____

ZIP/POSTAL CODE _____
Offer expires September 30, 1981.

102563371